# Kinky Boots

## K D GRACE

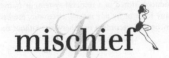

mischief

*Mischief*
An imprint of HarperCollins*Publishers*
77–85 Fulham Palace Road,
Hammersmith, London W6 8JB

www.mischiefbooks.com

A Paperback Original 2013

First published in Great Britain in ebook format by
HarperCollins*Publishers* 2012

Copyright © K D Grace 2013

K D Grace asserts the moral right to
be identified as the author of this work

A catalogue record for this book is
available from the British Library

ISBN-13: 9780007553334

Find out more about HarperCollins and the environment at
**www.harpercollins.co.uk/green**

# CONTENTS

| | |
|---|---|
| Chapter 1 | 1 |
| Chapter 2 | 15 |
| Chapter 3 | 24 |
| Chapter 4 | 34 |
| Chapter 5 | 43 |
| Chapter 6 | 54 |
| Chapter 7 | 62 |
| Chapter 8 | 71 |
| Chapter 9 | 86 |
| Chapter 10 | 99 |
| Chapter 11 | 114 |
| Chapter 12 | 135 |
| Chapter 13 | 150 |
| Chapter 14 | 159 |
| Chapter 15 | 167 |

# Chapter 1

A girls' night out with Vivie usually ended up a solo act for Jill. It always started with the best intentions, but then Vivie would hook up with someone hot, shag his brains out and call Jill all apologetic the next morning, or whenever the hangover wore off. Every time, Jill promised herself she wouldn't let it happen again. But she could never say no to Vivie.

This time they'd been separated at the Bluu Bar just off Hoxton Square. Jill figured Vivie and tall-dark-and-dressed-for-success – who had at least been polite enough to buy them both a drink before he whisked Vivie away – were probably occupying one of the benches in the square having a good grope. From there they would graduate to his flat or hers, possibly even the nearest alley if they couldn't wait that long. Vivie was a bit of an exhibitionist. Crowded into a standing-room-only corner next to the bar, Jill finished her wine then texted Vivie that she was going out for some air.

It wasn't supposed to be a late night. Her twat of a boss had informed her an hour before quitting time that he needed her to work tomorrow. More like he needed her to do *his* work tomorrow. He'd been sniffing around the new receptionist every chance he got. It didn't take a genius to figure their habitual two-hour lunch breaks had nothing to do with business or lunch. He boned the silicone-enhanced receptionist, and Jill got screwed.

Still, she was in Shoreditch on a Friday night. If she were going to end up alone, she couldn't think of any place she'd rather be. It was easy to get caught up in the excitement along the streets lined with bars and clubs and interesting shops. She loved the higgledy-piggledy architecture that often involved glass and steel in the personal space of very accommodating Victorian brick and stone that had already gone through who knew how many marriages of convenience before. All around, the concrete ugliness of the 60s groped and nuzzled solicitously at streets that could have come straight from a Sherlock Holmes novel. It was a great patchwork of a place, heaving with frenetic humanity all bound and determined to enjoy the hell out of every last drunken, chaotic, celebratory second of the weekend. She was jostled by the enthusiastic spill-over of people with drinks and fags in front of Juno. A hen party pushed past into an off-licence. People on the busy pavements crowded onto the narrow side streets, impeding the odd taxi or limo. Jill hadn't walked terribly far before she'd realised two things: her feet were killing her in the suicide shoes she'd borrowed at Vivie's insistence, and she was feeling very disoriented, not entirely sure where she was. She blinked and looked around to find herself wandering along Shoreditch High Street.

She half stepped and was half shoved into the entryway of a shop to avoid a handful of blokes in Chelsea football jerseys ambling by laughing drunkenly. As she leaned against the rough brick to slip out of the murderous shoes and wriggle her brutalised toes against the paving tiles, the irony wasn't lost on her that she found herself standing in front of a shoe store. *Kinky Boots*, the softly back-lit sign informed her in elegant gothic script. Underneath in smaller letters it read, *Wicked Vintage Shoes*. In spite of the late hour, the place was open.

She hadn't planned to go in. But when she leaned against the door, balancing herself to slip back into the vicious bite of the red stilettos, it swung open. Quickly she straightened herself and glanced around to make sure no one had noticed her less than elegant move. Then there was nothing to do but act like she intended to come right on in. And the thought of a cheap pair of comfy shoes to walk back home in sounded like a pretty good idea.

The shop smelled deliciously of well-worn leather and shoe polish with a bass note of strong coffee. Immediately she found herself nose to toe with a row of vintage-looking kitten heels flanked by a sexy display of thigh-high boots ranging in style from BDSM du jour to Goth on steroids to sassy sex goddess. She would be the first to admit that fashion was not her forte. But it was very much Vivie's, thus the enforced suffering of her aching feet.

'May I help you?'

She looked up to meet the questioning gaze of the store clerk, and couldn't hold back a little yelp at his unexpected nearness. He glanced at the killer heels, which she still held in one hand, then down at her feet and offered a knowing smile.

'Just thought I'd stop in for a look.'

She tried to slip gracefully back into the shoes, but he took them from her hand. 'Leave them off.' The slight gruffness of his voice was deliciously tactile, rubbing up against her like raw silk. 'I can see your poor feet need a break.' He motioned for her to follow him into the bowels of the store, right in deep, between the high racks of shoes and boots and sandals and mules and old and new and quirky and just plain strange. And in the midst of all the funky, freaky, fantastic footwear, there wasn't a single pair of trainers or Uggs or Crocs to be found. He guided her to sit in a Queen Anne chair upholstered in pale-blue chintz.

'Are you all right?' He knelt in front of her and sat the shoes down next to the chair.

'I'm fine,' she said. Then she offered a nervous laugh 'Other than my feet.'

He sat back on his heels. 'When women come in here alone at this hour, they've usually come over from Juno or the office after an argument with their bloke. Of course there are a fair few who've simply had enough dancing the night away in ill-fitting shoes.' He offered her a smile that made her feel warm down low in her belly. 'There's a reason I keep my shop open after hours on weekends.' He nodded down at her aching feet.

'It was a girls' night out,' she said. 'That's why I'm alone, I mean. We got separated.' He didn't need to know that her friend was getting shagged and she wasn't. 'These aren't even my shoes. I borrowed them from my friend Vivie.' She nodded down to the little red feet-killers. 'Well, she insisted, actually. And the skirt too.' She felt stupid for telling him that. Could she make it any more obvious that she was clueless when it came to fashion and dressing to impress the opposite sex?

He glanced fleetingly at the skirt, and she was suddenly aware of just how short it was, and just how much he could see from his position if he really tried. 'The skirt I like,' he said. 'However, wearing another person's shoes is not a safe thing to do.' The lines of his face hardened. His lips were suddenly set tight as though he were warning her about a serial killer on the loose. When he smiled up at her, his eyes reminded her of the sea that lapped at the cliffs around Tintagel: neither blue nor grey nor green, none of those colours, yet all of those colours.

The clerk lifted her right foot. She tried to squirm away but he held her firmly, flashing her a concerned glance from under a drawn brow. 'You could have seriously injured your feet walking around Shoreditch at night in someone else's shoes.'

The skirt she wore was a denim mini, and the way he sat between her legs made her feel exposed, vulnerable and something a lot more yummy. As he ran his thumbs up her instep and over the pad of her foot, she shifted in the chair, sliding down to accommodate his inspection.

'Shoes are so important. They protect our feet, our soles, the only part of us that regularly contacts the earth. They allow us that intimate connection with our planet while at the same time keeping us safe from it.' He continued his inspection of her feet, hands moving gently over her arch to the ball then to her toes as he cupped her heel in a warm hand. 'No two people's soles contact the earth in the same way.'

Her pulse thudded at the enthusiasm of his little speech, which, along with his gentle inspection of her feet, felt shockingly intimate, even more so than if he had actually peeked up her skirt. His actions were having a cumulative effect low between her hip bones. 'Maybe you could sell me something a little more suited to me.' Her words rushed out breathless and unsteady.

He placed both hands on his thighs and looked up at her. 'Did you have a pair in mind?'

She gave a quick glance around the store, and her eyes lit on a pair of mauve boots that came up just over the ankle, low on the calf. They sported delicate kitten heels and were threaded with sage-green laces that looked more like ribbons. 'How about those?' she said. Then she blushed fiercely. They were lovely, elegant and, any idiot could see, totally not suited for someone like her. 'Or maybe something a little more practical.' She avoided his gaze. 'A little less flashy.'

Ignoring her second thoughts, he stood and walked to the rack. She couldn't help noticing how nicely his butt filled out his jeans. She could imagine that arse had sold more than a few pairs of shoes to women who liked a good view. It was then she realised he had taken the boots straight off the display. 'I'm hard to fit,' she said as he knelt in front of her and unlaced one boot.

'Trust me –' he smiled up at her, opened the boot and offered it to her like Cinderella's Prince Charming '– I can fit you just fine.'

Everything in her went warm and liquid. Her breath caught at the feel of the leather as he guided the boot up over her heel. 'I've never felt anything so soft,' she said. 'And they're so pretty.'

'Shoes should be a sensual experience,' he said, moving his large hands up to cup her calf while he eased the boot into place. Then his agile fingers began to work the laces, plucking at them, caressing them, stroking them almost as though he were making music on them, like they were some exotic stringed instrument of leather and lace. And though she couldn't quite hear the melody, she felt the reverberation of his plucking and threading beneath the hem of the short skirt and all the way up into her warming panties.

'Nice, huh?'

It took her a second to realise he was responding to her response. God, was she actually moaning? And please, surely she wasn't grinding her bottom against the chintz. The blush flashed hot across her chest but then, instead of spreading to her face, it headed south, settling against her clit with a heated, unexpected nip. And her moan became a yelp, just a tiny one, but a yelp nonetheless. She would have apologised, she would have died of embarrassment and fallen completely through the chair, but he was already working on the other boot, strategically sitting between her legs, breath slightly accelerated, and … Surely she was mistaken. But as he shifted to cup her calf and smooth the second boot against her leg, there was no disguising the erection growing inside the front of his jeans.

Everything below her waist clenched in appreciation and she felt the heavy tingle of excitement up high between her thighs. The urge to rip aside the scrap of denim that was her skirt and the bit of satin that was her knickers, the urge to focus his attention somewhere far removed from her feet, nearly took her breath away. 'You like your work,' she managed, not actually looking at his crotch, but not actually looking away from it either.

'Very much,' he said, working the laces through his nimble fingers, making no attempt to hide his boner.

Was it her imagination or could she actually smell him now? It was not deodorant, not soap that she smelled but maleness. It was like baked bread and desert heat with some moist thick bass note that she felt at the back of her throat rather than smelled. It made her hold her mouth slightly open to take in the fullness of his scent, like a cat taking in the scent of a rival or a possible mate.

Was it her imagination, or could she actually feel his breath against the place where her thighs rested on the chair, teasing just at the edge of her skirt? The growing warmth she now felt in her knickers was definitely not in her imagination.

For a moment she closed her eyes, shutting out the precision movements of his fingers and the view of his body hunched almost protectively between her legs. Then she allowed herself to take in the picture of him that her other senses were painting so exquisitely. She heard the catch and slide of his breath, felt the velvet flutter of it raising goose flesh on the soft skin of her inner thighs. She inhaled the complex olfactory portrait of him, the scent emanating from his armpits, his pulse points and the place where his cock strained in its tight confinement. She could feel his skin on hers as his fingers brushed her calf. It all created a picture of him almost as vivid as the one she had seen.

She opened her eyes just in time to watch him carefully, precisely, rhythmically tie the bow in the lace of the second boot. And as he tugged the looped ends snug against the knot, she felt a ripple up both legs that accelerated and intensified as it raced up between her thighs. It continued along her spine, flashing red hot behind her eyes, leaving a plum-coloured after-image of the clerk's engrossed face.

She yelped and jerked in the chair, and the vertebrae in her neck popped. 'Did you feel that?' She was a hair's breadth away from tumbling into orgasm, and the man had done nothing more than lace her boots. He nodded, holding her gaze. His pupils were dilated, his breathing fast. For a second neither of them moved. Time itself didn't even move, like everything was holding its breath, like everything was waiting, just barely able to contain the anticipation, the excitement.

Then the world exploded back into real time, and she pushed her way out of the chair and onto the clerk who was still on his knees between her legs. He tumbled backwards against the floor with a guttural sound somewhere between a groan and a growl, and just managed to adjust his position as she ground her way onto his lap, straddling his groin. The skirt had ridden up over her hips, and the crotch of her panties was the only thing preventing her from rubbing her bare ache against the tell-tale bulge in his jeans.

Before he could say anything, she took his mouth in a clash of lips and teeth and tongue. He was more than accommodating, tongue darting, lips tugging in an effort that quickly escaped the confines of her mouth to nibble down over her jaw and wage a humid, ticklish assault on her nape, every nip of which she felt between her legs. He made quick work of her buttons, then pulled her blouse open and slid a bra strap aside to lift her right breast free to his cupping and kneading, free to be ravaged by his very expressive mouth. 'I shouldn't be doing this,' he whispered against her breast. 'Not during working hours.'

'But I need you,' she said, then gasped and shuddered as he bit her nipple. 'I'll never make it back home like this. Don't force me to take care of myself in an alley.'

'I'm supposed to be selling shoes, not shagging my customers.'

'You are selling shoes.' She wriggled her toes in her boots. 'See. And who says we have to fuck?'

He offered a wicked chuckle, then rolled with her, and when he was on top, he lifted her legs around his hips so that his still clothed erection raked between her still-panied swell. 'You're absolutely right. We don't have to fuck,' he said, looking down at her with his ocean-changeable eyes. 'I always try to satisfy my customers.' Then he shifted his hips until his girth pressed her panties tightly into her heat, the fabric binding with a little hitch right against the swell of her clit as he ground and thrust.

She scrambled to meet him with her own thrust upward, and when she did so, when her hips were off the floor, he slipped both hands into the legs of her panties from behind and grabbed her bum cheeks in kneading fistfuls.

She dug her booted heels in just above the waist of his jeans for a better grip.

His whole body was tight, ridged, like it might shatter with the next thrust. The tighter his body became, the more liquid was hers, until she feared she would dissolve into nothing more than a tidal pool of quivering relief.

Each time he thrust she raised her legs a little higher, like she was climbing his body. Each time she raised her legs, his grip on her bottom became more possessive, more demanding. The friction was maddening down where clothing rubbed against clothing, and what was underneath felt the heat like flint and steel waiting for the spark. And when the spark came, it ignited a flash fire that left them both growling and straining like animals. The orgasm that started between her legs snaked up her spine and short-circuited her brain just before it slid down all the way to the tips of her toes in her soft leather boots. Then it curled itself around her like a warm embrace and finally settled between her hipbones like something smug, like something self-assured, like something completely at home there.

After that, it all happened at once. Her BlackBerry buzzed with a worried message from Vivie. Where was she? Was she all right? The phone on the counter rang and the clerk, with his jeans now wet, scrambled to answer it.

'What do you mean Eleanor's missing?' He spoke in hushed tones while making an effort to straighten himself. 'You know what night it is. You were supposed to keep an eye on her. You know how she is.' His voice had become a hiss close to the receiver, though he forced an embarrassed smile in Jill's direction, trying to make her feel more comfortable, no doubt.

But she didn't feel uncomfortable. In fact, she felt rather delicious. She wasn't sure why his obvious stress didn't bother her. She wasn't sure why she suddenly felt like the cat who just ate the cream. And she wasn't sure why she wasn't second-guessing what had just happened. Instead she offered him a seductive smile, blew him an even more seductive kiss, turned in her lovely new boots and walked out the door. She didn't know why she ignored him when he slammed the phone down and called after her. And did she hear right? Did he actually call her Eleanor? How utterly strange.

Even though it wasn't a long walk from Shoreditch

High Street to her flat, she took a taxi. She was sitting in the back seat, still straightening and buttoning, when her BlackBerry buzzed again with another frantic message from Vivie. She texted back.

*No worries, love! Had totally fab time, & the fun is just beginning.*

*J x*

*PS*

*Bought sexy new boots.*

She giggled as she remembered she hadn't paid for them. No probs. It would give her an excuse to see the yummy clerk again. And next time she would fuck him. Hard.

She signed the text *E xx*

# *Chapter 2*

Jill returned to her flat feeling pretty chuffed with the events of the evening. Nice place, Kinky Boots. Really nice. And the bloke who ran it – hotter than hot. There was something else about him, something strangely familiar, almost like if they sat down together over a cuppa they'd discover that they'd always known each other. She smiled to herself at the thought. She really couldn't imagine them getting through a whole cuppa together without her ripping his jeans off and shagging him senseless. Even with his clothes on, it hadn't been hard to tell that he was very nicely equipped for the task. She looked down at her lovely new boots, boots she'd left without paying for. It was the perfect excuse for going back.

\* \* \*

Under the circumstances, she figured she'd be too hyped to sleep, but she did so almost instantly.

15

And before long the room was awash in mist that floated and swirled around her bed. Had the weather turned while she was sleeping, bringing the fog? Had she forgotten to shut her window? A sudden gust of cool wind cleared the mist just enough for Jill to catch the first glimpse of the woman at the foot of her bed, pale and translucent, lit with way more silver light than even the full moon could provide.

Strange, as she approached the bed, the curvy, feminine shape of her was clear, as though her thin clingy robe were made from the mist itself, but the woman's face remained out of focus, as though Jill were viewing her from underwater.

She sat down on the bed next to her, and still Jill couldn't make out the details of her face. But her voice was rich and silky, and Jill had the urge to wrap herself in the caress of it. 'I've waited a long time for you, Jill Hart. Finn is such a spoilsport, not letting me play. But you're different. He likes you, and he'll warm to the idea of the two of us. You'll see.' She rubbed her hands together in anticipation. 'Now then, sweetie, let's have a look. Let's see our lovely new body.' As she reached out to smooth Jill's hair away from her face, Jill was suddenly unable to move.

It was a dream then, surely a dream, Jill thought; one of those where someone important is at the door, but you're paralysed, lying there in the bed, and, no matter how hard you try, you just can't move.

The woman leaned down and kissed her on the mouth, and her breath was winter-cold but sweet and hypnotic with its icy in and out, in and out.

With a flick of her wrist she threw back the duvet and sighed her delight. Jill was surprised to find herself naked. 'Oh, my darling, how I've longed to bear the weight of breasts again, to feel the hardening and puckering of their arousal.' She brushed cold fingertips across Jill's nipples and they rose to a touch that was irresistible. Jill would have arched up against the cool feathery caress if she'd been able. Instead she lay unmoving, her chest rising and falling faster and faster, her nipples pearled to hard beads begging for the woman's attention.

The woman continued her explorations. 'Oh, the delight of belly and hips, and, ah, yes, such softness down there.' She trailed her fingers down Jill's tummy and cupped her mons, caressed and fondled her tight curls, and the sound that escaped Jill's lips was a kittenish mew.

The woman smiled knowingly. 'The pleasures of the flesh, my lovely, how we shall share them, how we shall revel in them, you and I. It'll be so delicious for both of us, I promise you.' Then, with the flat of her hand, she opened Jill's legs.

Jill was helpless to deny her access, even if she'd wanted to, and she didn't. It was only a dream, she told herself, and sexy dreams should come as no surprise after her encounter at Kinky Boots. And anyway, it had to be a dream because she was too shy even to undress in front of Vivie, and here she lay practically willing this woman to check out all that she had … down there.

'Let us see, my darling,' the woman cooed. 'Let us see you.' Jill watched helplessly as the woman forced her knees up and wide until Jill felt herself exposed, butter-cream slick and heavy.

'Yes, my love. That's it. Let me see what we shall have such delight in sharing. Oh, yes, lovely. So lovely.' With one hand still resting in Jill's pubic curls the woman lowered her face for a closer look. Then with a scoop and a twist she trailed fingers up between Jill's cleft and brought them to her lips as though she were tasting her favourite dish. 'Mmm,' she whispered. 'Oh, Finn's going to love you.' She lowered a tongue-flick of a kiss onto Jill's hard clit, and Jill came. The electrifying power of her orgasm raged through her paralysed body to every nerve ending, every blood cell, every synapse, raging out in all directions, then returning in a hot rush of energy to the hardened node of her clit before settling deep inside her. She could neither writhe nor buck. All she could do was moan and quiver.

'Oh, yes, my darling, you are delightful, the way your lovely pussy muscles tighten and convulse when you come. How wonderful it will be to have a body with such libido, such hunger. Oh, how Finn will ride you. I think that –'

The woman was interrupted by the call of a man. 'Eleanor? Eleanor, are you there?'

She put a finger to her lips. 'He'll find out eventually, dear Jill, but when he does it'll no longer matter.' She brushed a kiss across Jill's lips, and for the first time Jill got a clear view of the woman's face. She recognised it well because it was her face. Before she could dwell on the strangeness of such a revelation, the woman lay down in her arms, nuzzled in tight against Jill's breasts and pulled the duvet up over both of them. From a distance Jill could still hear the man calling for Eleanor, but that was the last thing she remembered until morning.

\* \* \*

Finn scrubbed a hand over his face, feeling poorly slept with. He hadn't been slept with at all, actually. He gulped back the bitter taste of coffee, which was about the only thing keeping him awake at the moment. In truth, it was the woman he'd been with last night who was keeping him awake, and not in a good way. She was nowhere to be found, and she could very well be in a great deal of danger. 'I've never seen her before,' Finn said. 'She stumbled into the shop, bought a pair of boots and left.'

'Did you fuck her?' Meinrad asked.

Finn tried to work up the energy to be offended by

Meinrad's bluntness, but he knew better. Meinrad was right to want to know. 'If I had fucked her then I'd be certain, wouldn't I? We'd know, wouldn't we?'

Meinrad's pale-blue gaze was a study in Teutonic seriousness. 'You must have done something or you wouldn't suspect that Eleanor's with her.'

Meinrad was so damn smug at times, and Finn really didn't need smug right now. 'I … we had a good grope.'

'How much of a grope?' Meinrad asked. 'Did she come? Did you come?'

'Yes, she came, and so did I, all right? And I shouldn't have. I mean I knew what day it was, but I thought you and Chelsea had Eleanor under control. How was I supposed to know she was out and about?'

Meinrad stopped sipping his coffee and blinked. 'She wasn't exactly out and about, mate. Besides, it was you who had the desire to grope a total stranger enough to jizz your jeans. That wasn't a clue?'

Finn stood and paced, then poured them both another cup of corrosive coffee. 'I don't suppose it ever occurred to you that the woman was really hot and that she might actually fancy me?' He dropped back into the chair slopping coffee, remembering the woman whose glorious dark hair looked like she'd just gotten out of bed after a sexy romp, and wouldn't he love to be on the receiving end of that romp? Then he added, 'Honestly, I wanted her from the moment she walked through the door, all barefoot with that pouty-lipped smile I could have eaten off her face.'

Meinrad gave him an unimpressed look. 'Sometimes it's best to keep your cock in your pants, Finn. If Eleanor's with this woman and her pouty lips, then you know the kind of trouble she can cause. The woman could be in real danger.'

'I know this, Meinrad. Don't you think I know this?' The thought had knotted his stomach since the moment the phone rang last night, and she sauntered out the door, disappearing into a birthday party stumbling drunkenly down the street from Juno. By the time he'd managed to push his way into the party, she was nowhere to be found. 'I've been using every means I can think of to find her.'

'If you haven't found her by now then it's already too late.'

'We don't know that, do we? It hasn't been twenty-four hours yet.'

Just then Meinrad's iPhone rang. He answered it with a grunt, then a nod, as though whoever was on the other end should be able to see. 'Right. Well, that's a start, isn't it?'

He hung up and offered Finn what could have been a smile or could just as easily have been a grimace. With Meinrad, it was difficult to tell. 'Chelsea found out who this Vivie is that your girl was talking about last night. You know, the one who lent her the killer shoes? Seems she was frantically looking for her friend Jill about the same time you were giving her the full frontal rub-up. Some bloke Chelsea knows, a banker she's fuck buddies with, was apparently doing the nasty with this Vivie in Hoxton Square and, after they'd done the deed, Jill was nowhere to be found. He happened to let it slip.'

Jill. Nice name, Finn thought. But what he felt was a sense of relief. If they had even a little bit of information about Jill, even her first name, if there were ways of finding her, then they could call in the rest of the Sole Alliance. If anybody could find Eleanor, they could. Of course once Eleanor had what she wanted, she wouldn't be hard to find. He shivered at the thought. He wished desperately he'd been more careful, that he'd just asked the woman out for coffee like a normal bloke would have. But then she did practically attack him, didn't she? Not that he wasn't willing. God, he had been willing.

'All right,' he said. 'Call everyone together. Let's find Jill, and hopefully Eleanor.' He left Meinrad sitting at the table calling in the members of Sole Alliance. He shoved open the door that separated his flat from Kinky Boots, made his way around the counter and through the racks of shoes and boots to the front of the store. For a second he stood looking out onto Shoreditch High Street. It was already heaving with traffic, but it was still too early for many shoppers to be out and about. With a sigh, he pulled down the steel shutters over the

22

storefront that he'd only opened a few minutes ago. Eleanor always was the queen of poor timing. Missing Saturday market business wasn't great, but there wasn't much choice under the circumstances. Jill had to be found for her own protection.

# Chapter 3

Jill woke up before the alarm went off. Thoughts of her encounter at Kinky Boots set off an eruption of butterflies in her stomach, and she couldn't keep from smiling as she saw the lovely pair of mauve boots sat neatly at the foot of her bed. Still unpaid for too.

The steamy shower felt like a million tiny massages all over her body and the loofah stimulated every pore of her pinkened skin to tingle with delight. It didn't even matter that, if it weren't for her boss, she'd still be enjoying a lie-in all snuggled under the crisp, clean duvet. In fact the morning seemed entirely too amazing to waste sleeping. Though the sleep last night had been particularly satisfying, and she seemed to recall very arousing dreams. Not too surprising under the circumstances, she thought. And as soon as she could placate her boss and get free, she hoped for a helluva lot more than just dreams.

Breakfast never tasted so good, even if it was only

toast with marmalade. She made the coffee stronger than usual and delighted in the bite of it against the back of her tongue, balanced by the velvet smoothness of the cream. In spite of her lack of interest in fashion, today it seemed a delicious chore to pick out just the perfect clothing. She chose a black pencil skirt, a soft silk blouse that was a riot of rich summer hues, and her lovely new boots. There was a bit more cleavage showing than usual, a bit more colour in the make-up. And the skirt, well, the skirt fitted like a glove. Though it came several inches below her knees, there was a long slit high up the right thigh. Under normal circumstances she would never have worn it to work, but she planned to pop by Kinky Boots afterward and pay her debt. With interest. Before she stepped out of the door into the early-morning chill, she pulled on the matching summer jacket and slipped her BlackBerry into the pocket.

To her surprise, when she arrived at the office, she found no one there but herself and her boss. It felt chilled and overly air conditioned without the complement of warm bodies crowded into the open-plan working space. She shivered and pulled her jacket tighter around her. The situation was almost enough to trash her post-coital morning. Being alone with the tosser always made her skin crawl, but the fact that she really was alone with him this time caused a cold clench in her stomach. She wondered what the hell was going on.

She went quietly to her desk, not wanting to draw his attention. With any luck he'd be too hungover to care what she did, then she could get her work done and leave. She spent an hour tweaking and cleaning up other people's articles and finalising the layout for that week's *Full On* webzine, tasks that he should have done. She was beginning to think she might get by unnoticed when she realised the article on street buskers she'd spent nearly a month researching had been pulled completely. It had been replaced as the lead story by an article on discount holidays lifted straight from an affiliate newsfeed. It wasn't the first time her boss had promised that her article would be the lead story, then pulled it at the last minute for no good reason. It would bloody well be the last, she decided. Breathing fire, she slammed her laptop shut, crossed the maze of cubicles to her boss's door and knocked before she had time for second thoughts.

He spoke to her without looking up from his laptop. 'You're upset about your busker story.' He didn't wait for her to respond, but continued. 'I made an executive decision, hon.' He took off his glasses and finally looked up at her. 'It just wasn't the kind of professional quality I'd hoped for, and when there was nothing else, I had to make a choice, didn't I?'

Her body stiffened. She stroked and clutched the BlackBerry in her pocket like it was a talisman. 'There was nothing wrong with that article,' a voice whispered in her ear. 'It was a good article, a damn sight better than what's up there now.' It was only the sour look of surprise on her boss's face that made her realise there had been no voice whispering in her ear. She had spoken the whole thing out loud, and she *certainly* wasn't sorry she'd done it!

'I believe the choice of what's good and what's not is mine to make, honey. The name on the door of this office is still H. Devlin, isn't it? Last time I looked it hadn't been changed to Jill Hart.' He pushed his chair back and came around the desk to stand in front of her, giving her a once-over that made her shiver. 'Nice outfit, by the way. I always suspected there was a nice figure under all that frump.' He moved closer, breathing stale coffee in her face, then he lowered his eyes to the buttons of her blouse and smiled conciliatorily into her cleavage. She pulled her jacket protectively around her.

'The wonderful thing about the web,' he said, 'is that we can change it, hon. Online publication is so much more forgiving than print. And one of the reasons I had you come in this morning is that I thought we might be able to get your article up as the lead story, if you're willing to work with me on it.' He straightened the collar of her jacket, pushed it back slightly and ran a finger along the open lapel of the blouse. 'You know, tweak it a bit here and there.'

'All right,' she said, tugging at her jacket and stepping

out of his breathing space until she could feel the wall against her spine. 'I'll go get my laptop, and we can work on it, though wouldn't it have been easier for you just to email me the changes you wanted? I could have done them from home.'

He stepped into her space again. 'I'm a hands-on sort of bloke, honey, and if you want your story to lead, then we'll have to work on it together.'

She stood very still, amazingly calm under the circumstances. He placed one hand on the wall just above her shoulder and the other pushed the jacket down over one arm and skimmed the open neckline of her blouse again.

'Is this what you had me come in for?' she asked.

He offered her a twitch of a smile. 'Oh, don't tell me you weren't anticipating it, honey. I mean, look how you're dressed.' Then his business voice returned. 'You're talented and enthusiastic, Jill. I can make sure that you go far in your career.' He leaned forward and his wet lips brushed her ear. 'Or not.'

She couldn't believe how calm she was. It was strange. There was no panic, no fear, no real rage even, just an icy distancing she never remembered feeling before. 'What do you want me to do, Mr Devlin?' she said above the strange buzzing in her ear, a sound not unlike the buzz of insects in a field on a hot summer day.

He chuckled, and his breath was heavy and damp against her face. 'There, that's better now, isn't it? I love a cooperative employee.' He slid a pudgy thumb across the outline of one nipple and sighed. 'First, I want you to lose the jacket, unbutton that lovely silk top of yours and give me a good look at those tits you're always pointing at me. And when I've had enough time to examine them thoroughly, I want you over my desk, skirt up, arse cheeks parted so I can have my choice of what you've got down there. Are we clear, honey?'

The buzzing grew louder. But strangely the world around her seemed sharply focused, more detailed than she could ever remember it being – the smell of cold coffee in a paper cup on his desk, the sound of a jackhammer on a nearby street, the tiny mole just in front of the man's right ear, the growing crescents of sweat beneath his armpits sharp with the acid scent of nerves overriding the citrus tang of deodorant. 'Oh, we're very clear,' she said, caressing her BlackBerry again. 'Clear as a bell.'

She placed the flat of her hand against his chest and shoved him hard. He gave a little grunt of anticipation, like maybe he was OK with a woman taking the upper hand. He had no idea, she thought. He stank of his own lust, and she could damn near read his mind. He thought he was in, he thought she was kinky enough to be turned on by him, the little toad. And when she'd pushed him back until his bum rested against his desk, he practically quivered with excitement. The laugh that came from her throat startled even her. The man was pathetic, and her time was way too valuable to waste on such a creature.

She spoke as calmly as if she had just told him the football scores. 'You disgusting little worm. Do you really think there's anything you could do to persuade me to let me put your filthy little cock inside me? You have two hands, Devlin, I would suggest you fuck yourself, and, while you're at it, fuck this job because I no longer need it.'

She heard the pop of joints as he catapulted off the desk into a stiff-necked stance, eyes bulging, chest inflating like a balloon. 'You filthy slut! Clear your desk, you little bitch. I want you out of my sight. Now!'

'Oh, don't worry, Devlin. I'm leaving.' She stepped back just beyond the range of his anger, and it really was as though her right hand didn't know what her left hand was doing. 'But before I go, you'll agree to make sure my unexpected leaving is nicely smoothed over with HR. You'll also make sure that I'm very well compensated for putting up with you, Devlin, very well. And finally you'll make sure there'll be the stellar references I deserve for my CV.'

'You fucking little bitch.' He lunged for her but she stepped back, pulled the BlackBerry from her pocket and hit the playback button.

*What do you want me to do, Mr Devlin,* Jill heard herself say. Then she heard her boss's fetid laugh.

*I want you to lose the jacket, unbutton that lovely silk top of yours and give me a good look at those tits you're always pointing at me ...*

When she switched the recording off, the man looked decidedly green.

'I think we understand each other, Mr Devlin. I'll be back Monday to pick up my things and talk to HR. What you do between now and then will determine what I do with this lovely little recording. Are we clear?'

The man nodded. In truth she was afraid if he opened his mouth he might just throw up.

'I know a lot of the women who work here, and I know how you treat them. I'll be having coffee with them from time to time, just to see how things are going. You get the picture.' She held up the BlackBerry. 'Oh, and one more thing, Devlin. My busker story leads this week's eZine, according to plan.'

Then she walked out of his office, shut the door quietly behind her and just kept walking with the strange buzzing in her ears reducing everything else to background noise. She felt like her head was too full, too full of everything, colour and light and darkness and texture and scent and sounds and distance and space and time. And everything felt so completely solid. Inside her there was a powerful urge to run down the street laughing hysterically. The job from hell was finished. Finished! She'd never have to face Devlin again.

Right next door to the urge for hysterical laughter was the urge to panic hugely. The battling urges threatened to rip her chest open, threatened to cut off her breathing, threatened to drive her to her knees. But the sun was bright and the air was warm and she was going to Shoreditch to fuck the clerk at Kinky Boots.

* * *

In the end Chelsea called her fuck buddy, the banker, who called Vivie. Because she fancied him, it hadn't taken him long to wheedle Jill Hart's name out of her. It turned out Vivie was a bit of a matchmaker and found the idea of hooking up her friend with a hot bloke irresistible. The hot-bloke bit was Chelsea's embellishment, not Finn's, but if it worked, it worked. By noon, Finn had tweeted and Facebooked Jill Hart. He was sure it was her because she had a fairly good photo of herself as her avatar. He'd got the number of her landline, but there had been no answer, and he'd had no response from his efforts with social media. Jill didn't seem like the type who would leave a debt unpaid. He was sure she'd be back once she realised that she hadn't paid him for the boots, but by then it could be too late. It was frustrating. It was more than frustrating, it was frightening. Eleanor had never deliberately hurt anyone. Not deliberately. But after the last time, Finn couldn't believe that she would

32

willingly do what she'd clearly done. The thought made him cold inside.

He was getting desperate when he got a call from the Water Poet pub. The bartender was a friend. There was a woman at the bar fitting Jill's description. She was doing tequila shots.

# Chapter 4

It was only when Jill was in the tube heading toward Old Street Station that the impact of what she had done hit her full-on. She probably would have collapsed in a heap, but the carriage was packed cheek to jowl. She had just quit her job! Christ! Not only had she quit her job, but she'd told her boss to fuck himself. She hadn't even realised she was recording the bastard. How could she not realise? If anyone else had done what she'd just done, she'd be congratulating them, patting them on the back, buying them a drink for giving the arsehole what he deserved. But it wasn't someone else. It was neurotic, shy, insecure and now unemployed Jill Hart who had done it. What the hell would she do now?

Instead of paying for the boots she could no longer afford, Jill ended up wandering aimlessly around Shoreditch silently arguing with herself amid the Saturday bustle of shoppers. The job, which she would have other-wise enjoyed, had been a nightmare from the beginning, and all because of Devlin. And now she had the man by the short hairs. She would have a bit of a cushion until she could find what she wanted. It was all so exciting, she tried to convince herself. She had just opened the door to all kinds of new possibilities. On the other hand, she had just opened the door to poverty and moving back home with her mother, a thought that made her queasy.

She wasn't sure how long she wandered about, or which part of her had won the argument, but when she finally came back to herself, leaning against the bar at the Water Poet pub downing her second tequila shot, she figured it was not Betty Bright-Side who had come out on top.

'Tequila before lunch is not a good sign.'

She was surprised to find the clerk from Kinky Boots standing next to her, if anything looking even sexier in the bright light of day than he had in the mood lighting of the shoe store. He ordered a coffee.

'What are you doing here?' she asked. 'Are my boots equipped with a tracking device for customers who leave without paying?'

He offered her a smile that seemed to turn inwards, as though he knew a private joke. 'Something like that.' Then he added, 'I figured you'd come back, and even if you didn't, I can hardly begrudge you the boots after … well, after such a lovely down payment.'

She laughed softly at her own private joke, but then

she decided not to keep it to herself. 'Afraid a down payment may be all you'll get. I just quit my job.'

'Oh?'

'My boss is an arsehole, OK, but that's nothing new. Up until now I've managed to get by keeping a low profile. But today ... don't know what came over me. Guess he finally just pushed me too far.'

The man's startling eyes darkened like a storm, and he leaned closer. 'What happened, if you don't mind my asking?'

She found that she didn't, which was strange. There was a time, only yesterday in fact, when what her boss had done to her would have embarrassed her, would have made her doubt herself and wonder what she'd done to make him think of her that way.

When she'd finished her story, the clerk's eyes had gone from stormy to a total cyclone of rage. The muscles along his jaws looked like he could chew bullets, and Jill noticed his fists clenching and unclenching at his side. 'Sounds like the bastard deserved what he got and then some,' he said. 'You shouldn't have had to deal with that.'

'Well, I did. And now I'm unemployed.' When she started to order another shot, he laid his hand on hers.

'Don't do that.' He held her gaze, and the feeling wasn't unlike looking over the cliffs into a raging sea. 'Since you can't afford to pay for the boots, I see no other option but to have you work off your debt, and you can't work off your debt if you're drunk.'

She blinked. 'But I don't know anything about selling shoes.'

Ignoring the fair-sized crowd of early lunchers and the press of loiterers at the bar, the clerk tilted her chin with the curve of a finger and brushed a tease of a kiss against her lips. Even though it was barely there, no part of her anatomy missed the flick of his tongue. When he pulled away, still holding her gaze, they were both breathing noticeably harder. She was suddenly aware of just how trimly the T-shirt with the electric-blue Kinky Boots logo fitted across his chest. 'Though it wouldn't be that hard to train you to work in the shop, what I had in mind is something that I hope you don't need any training for.'

'Oh. Oh!' There was something delightful, refreshing, regenerating in the fact that he wanted her still, even in the naked light of day, even with her miserable confession of unemployment. She responded by kissing him back, by answering his tongue with a flick of her own, by brazenly resting a hand high on his thigh. 'You'll have to excuse me, I don't get out much.'

'I like women who don't get out much. That means they're focused on things that matter to them, and I like that a lot.'

'Vivie calls that clueless,' she said breathlessly.

'I'm not Vivie, am I?' This time the kiss included an

embrace that jostled the drinkers at the bar next to them and nearly pulled her off her feet. He placed a warm hand against her bare skin, beneath the jacket and under the edge of her blouse. This time there was more than just a flick of the tongue, much more. And Jesus, did the man ever know what to do with his tongue!

Still ploughing her mouth like he expected to find hidden treasure, he fumbled in his pocket, pulled out a tenner and slapped it down on the bar. Then he pulled away for breath. 'Come on. Let's get out of here.'

They were only a few blocks from Kinky Boots, but it seemed too far. He barely had her out of the door before he crushed her to his chest and ravaged her mouth again, this time running both hands up under the back of her blouse, then down to cup her bottom and haul her up onto her toes until she could feel the rake of his growing hard-on against her pubic bone. He pulled away gasping, grabbed her hand and dragged her at a breakneck pace down Shoreditch High Street toward Kinky Boots. 'We'd better hurry,' he said. 'This time I don't intend to come in my pants, and I certainly don't intend for you to.'

Jesus, the man was talking dirty to her right out in the middle of the busy street. 'You're taking me back to the shop?' She balked. 'We're going to do it in a shoe store? On Saturday afternoon?'

He pulled her close and gave her another hard, quick kiss. 'Shop's closed. I'm taking you to my place.'

38

They rushed and pushed their way through the Saturday-afternoon shoppers and strollers. She was just barely able to contain the urge to elbow and stiff-arm people out of their way to clear a path when, at last, he led her through a maze of alleys to the back of a building. He unlocked the door and practically thrust her inside with his lips and tongue. One hand slammed the door behind them while the other shimmied the jacket off her shoulders onto the kitchen floor and made quick work of the buttons of her blouse before nimbly dispatching the hooks of her bra. That done, he gave a desperate kneading squeeze to each breast and a hard suckling kiss to each nipple, making her wet her knickers with delight before he returned his attention to her mouth.

'I dreamed about you last night,' he said, shoving her skirt up over her hips. 'I was trying to find you so we could finish what we started.'

'Me too. I dreamed about you.' She fumbled with his jeans, in an inelegant effort to free his cock, but he pushed her hand away impatiently. She watched in fascinated arousal as he unbuttoned and unzipped with one hand and, glory hallelujah, if the man wasn't commando! The swell of him spilled anxiously into his hand, ridged and weighty against the press of his balls and the pillow of dark russet curls beneath.

He rested one hand on his erection, almost like he needed to control it, almost like he were afraid it might get away from him. The other hand slipped aside the crotch of her panties. She thrust her hips forward and gave a little jerk of a gasp, banging her head against the wall at the startling pleasure of him parting the swell of her with two fingers. Then she yielded to his probing.

'Careful,' he said. 'I don't fuck the unconscious.' Then he let out a low whistle. 'Jesus, woman, you're so slick and soft. Once I'm inside you, I may never want to come out.'

'Once you're inside me I may never let you out.' She reached for his cock. 'Do it. I need you to do it. Now.'

Cupping his hands beneath her bottom, he lifted her as though she were weightless then pressed her back into the wall so she could shift her hips to open for his cock, so she could have the leverage to bear down and thrust back once he was inside her.

The power of his first thrust left her breathless. The girth of him felt as though it was forcibly spreading her hipbones apart. And when she was certain he'd rammed himself all the way up until he could touch the beating of her heart, he gave a soft grunt and held himself there, deep and tight, while she gripped and suckled and slicked herself down there, down between her thighs, in the painful pleasure of being so full, in the delicious effort to accommodate.

Then slowly, very slowly he began to withdraw, with her body grasping desperately as though it were making an effort to hold him there. All the way, he withdrew all the way, and they both cried out as though something had been ripped from them. Her throat ached from a growl that was barely human, and her body felt fevered and raw and so sensitive that she feared even a touch would abrade skin and bone. And yet she longed for so much more than just a touch. She could smell his animal-dark heat mixing with her own wet summer scent, making her wild with the want of him. Then he slid two fingers inside her and circled her clit with his thumb, never touching the rest of her, only circling, so close that she held her breath anticipating his conquest. All the while his dark seawater gaze was fixed on her face.

'I love that you're so wet,' he said nipping her throat just below her ear. 'I love that you're so ready for me.'

He held her there suspended, her legs still wrapped around him, her back still pressed tightly to the wall. The tip of his erection was almost but not quite touching her pout. It jostled and bounced while his fingers circled and probed and dipped until her clit felt like a small, hard mountain raised up by the circumnavigations of his thumb.

Just when she was certain she could no longer stand the heat, the sheer delicious friction of it, he thrust back into her. Hard! Fire shot up her spine and the buzzing returned to her ears, that same buzzing she'd had when she'd confronted her boss. She felt everything, every single pore of the clerk's skin where it touched hers, every hair follicle, every undulation of muscle, every sweep of breath. As the thrusting grew to a frenzy, he took her mouth with bruising force and when they were both so close to the edge that she was amazed he could speak at all, he forced the words out in a breathless hiss: 'I'm Finn, by the way.'

Finn? Where had she heard that name? It was familiar. 'Jill,' she gasped. 'I'm Jill.'

He bit her lip. 'And who else?'

She bit him back. 'Just Jill.'

This time the impact of his thrust felt like it would go clear through her and the wall behind as well. 'Oh, you're more than just Jill,' he managed. 'Way more.'

There wasn't time to question. There wasn't time for anything because they were there, on the edge, both tight and stretched and ready to shatter. He came first, but only by a breath. 'I'll ask you again,' he cried out. 'Who are you?'

It was only as she tumbled into orgasm that she realised, and she knew exactly who he was looking for. Even as the mother of all orgasms ripped through her, she was certain that not only was she not alone, but she hadn't been since she left Kinky Boots last night. In that instant, someone else borrowed her voice as though it belonged to her. That someone else said, 'I'm Eleanor, Finn, you silly man. You know who I am.'

# Chapter 5

As waves of orgasm convulsed her, last night's dream came rushing back to Jill in vivid detail. She felt like her brain was caught between channels, with visions of the woman sliding in and out of focus in her mind's eye, with memories of her touching her, exploring her, delighting in her. 'Who's Eleanor?' Jill gasped. 'What the hell's going on?'

Finn wrapped his arms tightly around her and held her, still fully impaled, still pressed against the wall. 'Jill, I'm going to pull out of you now. Just relax, stay calm and I'll tell you everything.' She might have been able to do as he asked if he hadn't, while still holding her gaze, said, 'Eleanor, I'd appreciate it if you'd cooperate.'

'Who the hell is Eleanor?' she asked again, struggling to stave off the rise of panic that wasn't supposed to be a part of post-coital bliss. But as he slipped out of her, as she felt their combine moisture trickle down the inside of her thigh in a warm rush, the rising panic slipped out of focus and hungry arousal slid into its place. She raked her fingers between her legs, then brought them first to her nose, then to her lips. 'Oh, my, how we taste together, Finn.' She repeated the action and brought the offering to his lips.

His eyelids fluttered, his groan was gut-deep as he lapped and suckled at her fingers, then he kissed her hard on the mouth, the aftertaste of them still on his tongue.

But this time Jill pulled away. 'My head, Finn! Jesus, what are you doing to my head? Did you see what I just did? And you just licked my ... and I feel ...' The rush of heat that snaked up her spine felt like it would fry her brain. 'I feel really strange,' she managed before her knees gave and the world spun around her. But even as Finn lifted her into his arms and carried her to the sofa in his lounge, she felt like she wanted to reach back between her legs again. She wanted to take Finn in her mouth and suckle and slurp until he was heavy and full and ready to burst again, and then she wanted him to thrust back into her, right back where she wanted him, where she needed him. To her horror, she realised that she had just expressed out loud those very thoughts and desires with words she'd never thought would ever come comfortably from her mouth.

'I'd like that too, Jill,' Finn responded. 'But not until I'm sure that's what you want, and not Eleanor.' He'd barely settled her onto the couch and managed to shove himself back in his jeans before the shakes hit, and she felt like they would break her apart.

But Finn pulled her into his arms and held her until they let up, then he tugged a blanket from the end of the sofa and placed it around her shoulders.

'Wait here and try to relax.' He disappeared into the kitchen and returned with a bottle of water, which she drank like she had been in the desert for a week.

He studied her for a long moment, then he heaved a sigh. 'Jill, what I'm going to tell you won't be easy to hear, but if you listen to me, if you pay attention, if you listen to yourself, you'll know that I'm telling the truth.'

'Who's Eleanor?' she asked again, feeling rude about being so blunt but not caring much under the circumstances, plus it was still an effort to keep her hands out of her knickers. 'And what's she doing inside my head?'

Finn scooted closer to her and tried to take her hand, but she pulled it away. The look that crossed his face was too swift to read, but he squared his shoulders and sat down, holding her gaze. 'Jill, Eleanor's a demon.'

Jill blinked twice. 'A what?'

He shifted and looked rather embarrassed, almost as though she'd just caught him masturbating in public. 'A demon,' he repeated. 'Eleanor's a demon.'

Before she could even laugh at the absurdity of Finn's statement, the voice inside her head said, 'Honestly, Finn, why do you always insist on using that word "demon"

45

when you know what it makes people in this day and age think? You make me sound like some sort of head-spinning, eye-bulging, pea-soup-vomiting monster or something, and I'm not like that at all, Jill. In fact, there was a time when the word "demon" meant something much nicer. It used to mean deity, divine power, lesser god, guiding spirit, take your pick, no head-spinning, no pea-soup-vomiting. That's just disgusting.'

Jill slapped her hand over her mouth, but it was too late. The words had indeed come out of her throat as quickly as they had come into her head. And they definitely weren't her thoughts. Her views on demons had always been pretty much bog-standard *Exorcist* stuff. Her views on demons! Hell, she didn't even *have* any views on demons. 'Oh, Jesus! Oh, God! Oh, fuck! You're joking, right?'

'Damn it, Eleanor, stop trying to help,' Finn said. And it was so bloody confusing because he was looking at Jill, addressing her, and yet the part that daintily gave him the finger was most definitely not her.

'Look, Jill,' Finn was now saying. 'It's not all that bad. Eleanor's right, she's not a demon like you think of in the *Exorcist* sense of the word. She's not anything like that. As far as demons go, well, Eleanor's not that bad. Really she's not.'

'Not that bad? Not that bad!' Jill was nearing hysterics. 'How can a demon be not that bad?'

'Well, it's like this ...' Finn laughed nervously. 'You see, there are lots of different kinds of demons and they aren't just evil or good, nothing that simple. It's a sort of continuum, if you know what I mean.'

'No, I don't know what you mean.' Jill pulled the blanket tighter around her and glared at him.

'Oh, for heaven's sake! Spit it out, Finn,' Jill found herself saying. 'I'm a lust demon.'

And bloody hell, the second she'd said it Jill's nipples were as hard as pebbles and she felt as though raw heat was scorching the crotch out of her knickers. She noticed immediately that Finn's cock was standing at full attention in his jeans.

And just like that, without giving it a second thought, Jill slapped him. She slapped him hard enough that she was sure it hurt her hand at least as badly as it hurt his cheek. 'You shagged me because of her, you bastard!'

It pissed her off that she heard Eleanor chuckle inside her head. It wasn't funny. She was really angry.

Finn recoiled from the impact, sucked a harsh breath, then sat rubbing his rosy pink cheek, eyes watering. 'I didn't! I wouldn't! I swear to you, when we were together last night I had no idea Eleanor was on the loose, and it was totally you that I wanted.'

'And today?'

He shifted nervously on the sofa.

'It was still you I wanted. It was just that ...'

47

'Just that if I were in residence and he did you, he'd know for sure I was there,' Eleanor said.

Jill slapped him again.

This time he recoiled with a curse. 'Goddamn it, Eleanor, stop trying to help.'

'So if she wasn't in me at our gropefest last night, then when?' Jill asked.

'The boots,' they both said at the same time.

'She came into me when I put on the boots,' Jill added, and in her mind's eye Eleanor nodded confirmation.

'How could this happen?' Jill said. 'I mean, all I did was come into Kinky Boots. I never even planned to buy anything. And really, me a suitable home for a lust demon? I mean come on. I can't even dress myself without Vivie's fashion advice.'

Inside her head, Eleanor practically doubled over laughing, and Finn wasn't much better. 'Are you kidding?' he said. 'Jesus, woman, you're sex on heels. In those boots, in Vivie's fuck-me shoes, hell, even barefoot, it was all I could do to keep from sucking your sexy bare toes and licking my way up from there.'

Inside her head, Eleanor positively purred.

'I'm possessed by a lust demon,' Jill said. 'This is hardly funny.'

'Look, I'm not laughing about that, Jill,' Finn said, forcing a serious face. 'Believe me, I know this is serious, but I agree with Eleanor. You're an obvious choice.'

'You knew about her?' Jill asked.

'Yes, I knew about her. In a way I suppose you could say she's my ward,' Finn said.

The voice in her mind offered a disparaging grunt along with a couple of choice invectives, spoken in quiet ladylike tones, of course.

'Your ward? Well, Finn, I'd say you're not doing a very good job keeping track of your ward, are you?'

'Oh, but I'll be ever so easy to keep track of now that the two of us are together, Jill,' Eleanor said.

'Eleanor's the last of the lust demons, as far as we can tell,' Finn said. 'And I'm not exactly her minder. It's more like an agreement between equals. It's an agreement between her and the Sole Alliance, an arrangement I was able to broker. So naturally when anything goes wrong, I get the blame for it.'

'Oh, poor you,' Eleanor said. Once again it was only Finn's raised eyebrow that made Jill aware she'd spoken out loud.

'Sole Alliance?' Jill asked. 'What's a Sole Alliance?'

'They're a nasty coven of mean witches and rabble intent on spoiling my fun.' Again Eleanor spoke out loud.

'Bloody hell, can't you make her stop doing that?' Jill said. But before Finn could respond, she said, 'A coven of witches? Oh, give me a break! What's next, ogres and trolls?'

'Don't be ridiculous,' came Eleanor's response, 'there are no ogres and trolls, at least not in London.'

'Make her stop that, damn it!' Jill fought back the urge to get hysterical. 'And get her out of me. Being possessed is not on the list of ways I planned to screw up my life. You get the blame from this Sole Alliance coven thingy, and now I'm blaming you too. I want her out. Can you do an exorcism?' Even as she said it she felt as though someone had just hurt her feelings in the most inconsiderate way. 'Look, I don't want to upset you, Eleanor –' and sure enough, she'd said it out loud '– but you came uninvited. The one thing I don't need in my life right now is a demon.' The word felt strange as it slipped from her lips, and she felt like a part of her was suddenly pouting. Then she turned her attention back to Finn. 'This is crazy. I don't know what's going on or how the hell you know about demon possession and all, or how you know about this Eleanor, but I want her out, do you understand? I want her out.'

Strangely enough, Eleanor made no comment, and for the moment, at least, Jill felt alone in her head. Before she could dwell on it there was a knock on the door, and a man the size of a mountain shoved his way in followed by a woman who was his total opposite, tiny and small of bone.

'This is Chelsea and Meinrad, the rest of Sole Alliance,' Finn said.

Meinrad, who had an unruly mane of white-blond hair and a colourful network of dragon and Celtic-knot tattoos ascending from his ham-hock-sized hands up both enormous biceps, gave her a nod and a grunt. He dwarfed her in his nearness, and in that close encounter it was easy to see there wasn't an ounce of fat on the man.

The tiny Chelsea was as dark as he was pale. She wore her hair in dreadlocks that hung to her shoulders, and her small braless breasts pressed enthusiastically against a thin green T-shirt. One hand was covered in silver rings, and one wrist was armoured in bangle bracelets halfway up to her elbow. She squeezed in next to the big man and nearly crushed Jill's fingers in her firm handshake. 'Pleasure,' she said in a gravelly voice that sounded as though it should belong to a much larger, much rougher-looking woman. 'We're here to do the exorcism,' she added. Then she offered a tight-shouldered shrug. 'Hopefully it's not too late.'

Before Jill could question further, Chelsea motioned to her to get up. 'Come on, come on. Time's wasting. Meinrad's prepared the space. If we're gonna do it, we need to do it now.'

Finn helped Jill to her feet and before she knew it Meinrad had thrown open a door next to a bookcase full of leather-bound volumes, a door she could have sworn hadn't been there before. The next thing she knew, she was being led down a steep wooden staircase into a cavernous cellar that looked hewn out of solid rock.

'Normally we would have a full coven, but the rest of the gang is on summer hols,' Finn explained, as though it were just a part of everyday conversation. Oh, the rest of the gang couldn't make the exorcism tonight. Shame, really, them missing out. Christ! Had she just dropped into Nutterville?

'Eleanor's usually quite well satisfied with sharing the three of us,' he continued. 'I don't know what came over her last night.'

'Full moon,' Meinrad said. 'That's what came over her.'

'She shares the three of you?' Jill said. 'As in possesses all of you?'

Meinrad blinked and looked at her as though she had just asked the stupidest question ever. 'Not at the same time.'

There were candles all around the room – black and silver. And in the middle of the space there was a heavy wooden table that looked like it could seat a dozen people. The table, however, wasn't set for Christmas dinner. It contained only a pewter chalice and a mean-looking bone-handled dagger. Finn moved close to her and slid an arm around her shoulder. 'Jill, we need you to lie down on the table.'

'Fuck!' A wave of cold fear struck her hard in the chest and the hair on the back of her neck stood up.

With a yelp of panic, she broke and lunged toward the stairs. No way was she being the sacrificial lamb! But Meinrad blocked the way, and running into Meinrad was like running into a solid wall.

Finn followed her gaze to the knife on the table. 'Oh, for heaven's sake, Jill, you can't really believe that …' He ran a hand through his hair and then picked up the dagger. 'It's an athame, a ceremonial knife used in magic, and trust me, it won't be used to draw blood.'

Chelsea offered her an elfish smile that was probably meant to reassure her, but it felt just this side of laughing at her. 'No human sacrifice necessary, we promise.'

Then Meinrad moved forward until she was once again nose to chest with him, and finding it impossible not to notice that the flexing of tattooed biceps made the dragons appear to be breathing. 'Look, do you want to be rid of Eleanor or not? Because time's wasting.'

'I do,' Jill said. 'Of course I do.'

'Then lie down on the altar and let us get on with it, will you?'

# Chapter 6

Feeling self-conscious and still not overly keen about the mean-looking dagger, Jill did as she was told. When she was flat on her back, Finn smoothed the hair away from her face and smiled down at her. 'Don't worry, Jill. It'll be all right.' He was so sincere, so why didn't she believe him?

She'd had nothing to eat since breakfast. She felt groggy, disoriented, as though she were experiencing the world through a fog. She doubted the tequila had helped the situation much, and she was thankful that Finn had stopped her before the count of shots had escalated. But then again, how sober did she really want to be for an exorcism?

The three members of Sole Alliance were saying some strange stuff about the four directions, and something about calling in the powers that lived in those directions, and Finn raised the bad-arse knife over her head. It was possible that she might have screamed – just a little – before he calmed her with a soothing touch and put the athame-jiggy aside. When the stuff about the four directions was finished, Chelsea passed the pewter chalice around, and everyone had a sip of whatever herby-smelling concoction was inside. Jill felt like she was being bathed in champagne with bubbles effervescing and bursting all around her, and the majority of them were nuzzling and caressing her still-aroused pussy.

Then the chanting began. She thought they were speaking English, and yet she couldn't understand a word. She couldn't focus. She couldn't think. She might have drifted in and out of a weird dream state, a state in which she felt as though she were lying on the table in the arms of a woman. She woke with a start expecting to find Chelsea nuzzled up against her, but Chelsea was still in her place, standing at Jill's left side, her eyes closed, her lips moving rapidly. And yet Jill felt the strange embrace. She could see Finn standing at the head of the table, looking down on her. She could hear his voice in the chanting chorus, and it sounded somehow like there were more than just the three of them. It made no sense, and the woman's embrace was still there, pillowing her head against soft full breasts that she found herself longing to suckle and caress. But there was no one there, only her, laid out on the table like an insane person.

Insane she might be, but she could see every bead of sweat breaking on Meinrad's forehead. She could see the shape of his erection straining to attention in his trousers, and she couldn't help wondering if it were in proportion to the rest of him. She had a feeling that it was. In fact she was certain of it, though she didn't know how she knew. And she didn't know how she knew that it was thoughts of plunging into her that were making him so hard and uncomfortable. Jill had to admit the thought of riding something so big was not at all unpleasant.

The smell of arousal was all over Chelsea and, though Jill was certain Chelsea had had both men in the past, it wasn't desire for either one of them that was exciting her at the moment. Jill knew the woman wanted desperately to lick her, not just to taste the arousal of another woman – Jill was pretty sure she'd done that lots of times – but it was Jill she wanted to taste, Jill she wanted to eat. And frankly, she wouldn't mind, not even a little bit. Had she ever been turned on by a woman before? She didn't think so, but then she'd never really thought about it. Still, it was easy for her to imagine kissing those lovely tight breasts, small and high and no doubt the colour of rich milk chocolate. In fact, she really didn't need to imagine. She knew.

But it was Finn who was definitely the centre of Jill's attention. He was having a very difficult time concentrating on the task at hand. His erection was about to burst his fly, and she knew that cock intimately. And wanted it. In spite of her best efforts to lie still on the table and mentally take in the weight of the fact that she was undergoing an exorcism, she was horny as hell, and dignity was not an easy thing to maintain.

It was Meinrad who finally broke the chant. 'Damn it, Finn, Eleanor's being stubborn. It's up to you to coax her out.'

'What does that mean?' Jill asked. 'Why is it up to Finn?'

'Because he's the one she trusts the most,' Chelsea said.

Finn came to her side and took her hand in his. 'Jill, that means we might need to get very intimate, are you all right with that?'

She wanted to say no. She wanted to be indignant. After all, none of this had been her idea, none of it had been her fault, and yet she wanted him so badly she could barely stand it. She pulled him down to her and kissed him savagely, tonguing his hard palate and running a hand down to stroke the straining of his erection through his jeans. 'If you need to fuck me, Finn, I'm OK with that,' she said. Even before the words were out of her mouth and he slipped onto the table next to her, she wondered how she could be so nonchalant about having sex with this man, a man she barely knew, with an audience she knew even less. And yet she felt like if he didn't mount her soon, she'd rip off her panties and take herself right here in front of them all. Was Eleanor making her feel this way? It didn't seem like it. It seemed like it was all her, all the pent-up sexual frustration of so many years of never having time for sex, never having confidence to seek out a partner, and now she wanted it. She wanted it badly.

She lifted her bottom and allowed Finn to slide off her knickers. And, as he pushed her legs open, everyone got a glimpse of her down there where she was hot and needy. Why wasn't she embarrassed? She opened her blouse and worried her bra cups down so her nipples peeked over the top like two hard little marbles. All the while she watched, anticipated, as Finn unzipped and untucked and shoved his trousers down until she could grab his bare bum as he positioned himself. And they were watching – Meinrad with his monster cock and Chelsea with her tight little breasts. Jill wondered if they could hold off and continue to chant all official-like while Finn took her. She bet they couldn't.

For a second she thought it was Chelsea making the little gruntings, the little girl-like whimperings and whinings, but it was her. It was her lifting her bottom, holding herself open with two fingers, raking at herself like there was no tomorrow. It was her, certain beyond a shadow of a doubt that if Finn didn't fuck her soon, she'd die, sacrificial lamb or not.

And when he wriggled into position and pushed up tight against her begging pout, she quivered all over in anticipation. She knew what he felt like. Dear heaven, she knew what he felt like, had known what he felt like for a very long time. He was the reason she stayed, the reason she agreed to their silly little pact, the reason she wanted flesh and blood and breath to channel her lust.

With a harsh grunt he pushed in, and Jill surfaced from a pool of thoughts that weren't hers, from feelings that were in themselves almost enough to make her come. And Finn began to thrust.

He was saying something. It wasn't a chant. It was something she should probably listen to, would probably have been able to if his pubic bone hadn't raked her clit so deliciously every time he thrust.

'Eleanor, please,' he was saying. 'You have to come out of Jill. She didn't ask for you. I promise, if you do, you can be in me as much as you want.'

Jill wrapped her legs around his hips, grabbed his hair and pulled his mouth down to hers. 'I don't want to be inside you, Finn Masters. I want you to be inside me. Don't you understand?' Had she said that? It certainly was true, wasn't it? She wanted the man to shag her brains out. She reached to grab his butt and pull him closer, deeper into her, and he groaned.

'Eleanor, please,' he whispered breathlessly between ravishing kisses. 'Jill didn't invite you. You're going where you weren't invited. Please don't do this.'

In peripheral vision that was somehow clearer and brighter than she ever remembered, Jill could see that

Meinrad did indeed have equipment proportionate to his body and it was now jutting from his open fly, shoving, bloated and stiff, in and out of the man's fisted hand, and he was still chanting.

On the other side of the table, Chelsea had a hand under her T-shirt pinching and tugging a nipple while she rode the other hand like she was a cowgirl on a bucking bronco. But she was still chanting in unison with Meinrad.

'Eleanor, please, please don't do this, not if Jill doesn't want it,' Finn said, nuzzling against her throat, speaking in harsh, breathy rasps. 'Please set her free.'

Jill could no longer distinguish where she left off and Eleanor began. The lust she felt was white-hot, but there was more, there was so much more. She could feel the demon down under her breastbone, up along her spine, underneath her skin and coursing through her veins. Eleanor was everywhere, Eleanor was everything. Eleanor was raw, aching power wrapped in a need that was unlike any need Jill had ever experienced. She stood only on the edge of the ocean of Eleanor, the ocean that was somehow, incredibly, impossibly, contained by her.

Orgasm came from a long way off, like a wave growing on itself. Jill wasn't sure where she was in that ocean of lust, but on it was a life raft, and that life raft was Finn. And if it were possible, he was filling her even fuller than Eleanor was. She held on tight, thrusting hard. Meinrad grunted his orgasm onto the floor next to the altar. Chelsea keened out her release against the press of her palm.

And then the world exploded outwards. Finn came. Jill came, and Eleanor curled around her in an embrace that was ecstatic and primordial and completely and totally new. And just at the instant before it all slipped away, Jill held on tight.

# Chapter 7

When Jill came to, she was lying on Finn's sofa. He sat on the coffee table next to her, bathing her forehead with a cool cloth. The relief on his face expanded to a cautious smile. 'Welcome back. You all right?'

Was she? She wasn't sure. Nothing seemed broken or damaged. Her head didn't hurt, and it was still on the right way. There was no urge to vomit pea soup. Her stomach felt just fine, though she realised she was ravenous. And damned if she still didn't feel like she could open her legs and pull Finn right down on top of her. He was certainly well equipped for it, with a hefty hard-on snugged up tight against the front of his jeans.

It was when she rested her hand upon it, when he moaned and bit his lip, that she noticed Meinrad glaring at her from across the room, arms folded over his deep chest as though he were standing guard. Chelsea sat on the arm of the sofa at her feet, leaning anxiously forward.

Then it all came rushing back to her, the altar table, the bad-arse dagger, the chanting, the sex. Eleanor.

She felt warm breath against the fine hair at the base of her neck, then it moved over the tips of her nipples and, like the brush of a feather, it flicked down her sternum and ended with a tiny puff against the node of her clit. As the pleasure of it rushed up her spine and straight to her brain, she knew.

'It didn't work,' she said.

Meinrad growled. 'You fucking have to want it to work first. She can tell that, you know?'

'Don't tell me what I want.' She forced herself into a sitting position, thought better of it as the world spun around her, and Finn eased her back down. 'You don't know what the hell I want. And don't go acting like it's all my fault you screwed up.'

'Ease off, Meinrad. Now.' Finn came to his feet so quickly that Jill had to do a double take. Almost before she could blink he stood nose to nose with the big man. 'Eleanor was in your care. You were her host.' He shot Chelsea a sharp look. 'Both of you.' The room practically vibrated with Finn's anger, and Jill felt something as visceral as it was sexual, laced with fear and the effervescent tingle of magic she'd felt on the altar.

'The two of you knew I was working in Kinky Boots, and you knew what night it was. What the fuck happened?'

It was almost as though Meinrad visibly deflated. 'I have no idea.' He plopped down in a partner to the Queen Anne chair that was in Kinky Boots, dwarfing it beneath his heavy haunches. 'Chelsea and I *were shagging*. We thought Eleanor was fully engaged. She was in me at the time. You know how she likes my cock.'

Jesus, too much information, Jill thought, but she was the only one who seemed to notice.

Chelsea nodded sagely. 'Usually Meinrad's size can keep her occupied for hours.'

Even Finn nodded his agreement.

'Like I said, Chel and I were shagging. She had just had a nice big come, and I was getting close.' The big man ran a hand through his wild hair. 'Well, you know, at that point a person's a bit distracted, a bit vulnerable. Anyway, I came, and before we caught our breath, we realised Eleanor was gone.'

Jill eased herself into a sitting position, and just when Finn was sure she was comfortable, the pizza arrived. 'Pizza after a botched exorcism?' She said. 'Who knew?'

'Food after magic,' Finn corrected, offering her a hefty piece of *quattro stagioni* on a plate Chelsea had scrounged from the kitchen.

'It wasn't a botched exorcism,' Meinrad said. 'It was a shot in the dark to begin with.' He seemed a lot less belligerent, almost apologetic. 'I'm sorry, Jill, but we all knew that going in.'

'So now what?' Jill spoke with her mouth full, wondering how she could be wolfing down pizza at a time like this, but God, it was delicious!

'She may come out on her own eventually,' Chelsea said, forcing a cheerful smile.

'Eventually?'

'If she gets bored or finds someone else more interesting,' Meinrad said.

'Lovely. So all I have to do is bore her.'

'I wouldn't hold my breath on that one,' Finn said, looking like he'd much rather eat her than the pizza. He moved to the couch, sat next to her and held her gaze. 'Jill, Eleanor was drawn to you because of your powerful libido. She was able to possess you because we were … intimate. The full moon made it easier for her.' The muscles along his strong jaw tensed, and he looked away. 'I'm sorry, I should have known not to …'

'It wasn't your fault,' Jill said. 'I practically attacked you.' She shot the other two a quick glance, daring them to comment. They didn't.

'She sensed you when you entered the shop, maybe even before, and she was already in the boots waiting,' Finn said. 'She's a lust demon. She's drawn to sexual chemistry, and ours had to have been off the scale. Plus the act of lacing, tying, binding, making knots is in itself powerful magic. Once I finished lacing both boots, she was right there and ready.'

'But why?' Jill said, already grabbing for her second slice of pizza. 'If she was in Meinrad at the time, and if he and Chelsea were shagging –' she couldn't hold back a blush '– then why wasn't that enough?'

'Sole Alliance is temporary housing,' Finn said. 'That was the agreement. She was to use our bodies when she needed them, and we were to make ourselves available. That was how we convinced Eleanor to … behave herself.'

Jill felt a chill. 'Behave herself?' As much as she hated to ask, she needed to know. 'Just what happens when Eleanor doesn't behave herself?'

The overburdened chintz chair creaked as Meinrad shifted uncomfortably. 'She possesses people, has lots of sex and, though she doesn't really make them do anything they don't want to, she strongly encourages them to do things that they might think twice about if she wasn't in residence.'

'It's all about physical experience for Eleanor,' Chelsea said. 'Being a demon and all, she has no body, so she misses out on the pleasures that come with it, like sex and hot baths and eating.' She nodded at the pizza. 'That means a body she can hang out in twenty-four-seven allows her the full experience, something Sole Alliance doesn't offer.'

'Eleanor wants the body she's in to feel really good,' Finn said. 'That means her host will be anxious to keep her in residence. The problem is the host doesn't always know what's really good, and the other side of Eleanor is all about finding those dark desires in the psyche that the host might not act upon without a little push.'

Jill shivered. 'Like attacking the shoe-store clerk.'

'Thing is,' Finn said, moving a little closer to her, almost as though he were afraid she might bolt, 'Eleanor, because she resides in you now, will know your darkest sexual fantasies better than you do, and she'll find a way to offer them to you, to make them real. Sometimes that's not a bad thing. Sometimes it can be very good.' He held her gaze. 'But it can also be dangerous.'

Jill's stomach knotted hard. 'I've already quit my job. I've bought boots I can't afford. I've had unprotected sex twice. I'm still horny as hell and it's been less than twenty-four hours. How am I going to survive living with Eleanor until she gets bored and decides to come out?'

'Sex is never unprotected when you're possessed by a demon,' Meinrad said. 'Eleanor wants your body safe and healthy so she can enjoy it.'

'Well, that's something, at least,' Jill said.

Finn took her hand in his. 'I won't leave you alone with her. I can sleep on your sofa or your floor if that makes you feel more comfortable.'

A stupid thing to say, she thought, since she'd already fucked his brains out twice. 'The rent's paid till the end of the month. After that you may have to share my park bench.'

'You won't need to sleep on a park bench, Jill. We'll see to that,' Finn said.

'Yes, we'll see to that.' A voice spoke inside her head. It was the first time she'd been fully aware of Eleanor since the failed exorcism.

Then she remembered the run-in with her boss, and a chill ran down her spine. 'My BlackBerry. The recording. Where's my BlackBerry?'

Jill pushed herself off the sofa and fled to the kitchen, where someone had hung her jacket neatly over the back of a chair.

Sure enough, she found her BlackBerry in the pocket. There was a text from Vivie asking what her plans were for the night. She ignored it.

'What's going on? What are you doing?' Finn called from the doorway, where he'd followed. Meinrad and Chelsea crowded in next to him as Jill hit playback and her voice filled the room.

*What do you want me to do, Mr Devlin?* Jill heard. She fast-forwarded until she heard her boss say:

*Unbutton that lovely silk top of yours and give me a good look at those tits you're always pointing at me. And when I've had enough time to –*

She stopped the recording, relieved that it was still there, that she hadn't imagined it, and embarrassed that all of Sole Alliance had heard her humiliation.

Finn moved to her side. 'That son of a bitch!' He slid a

protective arm around her shoulder. 'Good thing you had the presence of mind to record him. You'll have Human Resources eating out of your hand and that fucker will be lucky to work at McDonald's'

Jill shivered. 'I didn't have the presence of mind to record him.'

She'd barely got the words out of her mouth before Eleanor spoke. 'Oh, but you did. Trust me, darling, you didn't do anything you didn't have a deep-seated urge to do already. I just cheered you on a bit.'

Jill was suddenly trembling again. 'And the things I said? What I did?'

'You were totally in the driver's seat, Jill,' the voice in her head said. 'I wouldn't deprive you of that pleasure.' There was a soft laugh. 'If I had been in the driver's seat, we would have kneed the bastard nice and hard in the balls, and with strong, well-muscled legs like yours I reckon he wouldn't have forgotten us for a very long time. Goodness! For a second there I sounded almost like a vengeance demon, didn't I?'

Jill became aware of Meinrad and Chelsea staring at her as though she had two heads. Not that far from the truth, she thought.

'What, Jill? What's going on?' Finn asked.

'We're discussing who's in the driver's seat,' Jill said.

A look of disbelief passed between Meinrad and Chelsea. 'She's talking to you? Eleanor's talking to you?'

Meinrad said, as though the whole idea were shocking.

Jill nodded. 'Why?'

Chelsea stepped forward into the room. 'Because the only one she ever talks to is Finn.' She looked up at Meinrad. 'The two of us, we know she's there, and it's always obvious what she wants, but she never actually talks to us.'

Jill suddenly felt weak-kneed. Finn pulled out a chair and guided her into it. Inside her, it felt as though Eleanor was settled in comfortable silence, the kind of silence shared between two really good friends. That in itself was disconcerting, especially as the last memories of the failed exorcism came back to her strong and clear. Now that it was over, now that it was all safely behind her, she vividly recalled hanging on for dear life just before she lost consciousness, hanging on as though what was about to happen was something she couldn't let slip away. She was possessed by a demon, for God's sake! How could it be that she wanted to hang on? And yet there was no denying that she had. In her head Eleanor placed a finger on her nose like they'd been playing charades, like Jill had just won the game. There was a smile and a laugh that no one heard but her, and, though Jill figured it should be otherwise, Eleanor's presence felt completely comfortable.

# Chapter 8

With his rucksack slung over his shoulder, Finn followed Jill up to her flat on the seventh floor. The tour took thirty seconds. The flat was only slightly more than a studio, with a small bedroom and a bathroom off from the open living area. Jill had stretched herself to be able to afford it, and had lived very frugally in order to have her privacy. The possibility of losing her little island of solitude was one terrifying thought among many in the madness that stretched endlessly before her. She forced a smile as the two stood facing each other in the centre of the makeshift lounge. 'Home sweet home.'

'It's nice,' he said. 'It suits you.'

'Drink?' she asked. 'Wine, beer, coffee, tea?'

Finn shook his head. 'Nothing for me. It's late.' He put his rucksack down at the end of the sofa. 'Do you have a blanket or something? I'll sleep on the couch.'

The words felt like a slap in the face. Sleep wasn't really what Jill had in mind.

It was as though he'd read her thoughts. 'You've had a rough day, Jill, and you're exhausted. You don't realise it at the moment. That's what having Eleanor in residence does to you. But even she understands that in order to keep her host healthy, rest has to happen.' He tilted her chin, forcing her to meet his gaze. 'I've had her in me, Jill. I know what I'm talking about. I know how she is, what she can do to you.'

Jill's tummy gave a tight little quiver at the thought of the very feminine Eleanor, nestled in some inexplicable part of her, residing in that same inexplicable part of the very masculine Finn. But before she could follow that intriguing train of thought, Finn brushed a kiss across her lips and nodded to her room. 'Now go to bed. The next few days will be very demanding.'

Sullenly she brushed her teeth and took off the make-up she'd put on hours ago before she'd quit her job, back when the only thing she had to worry about was impressing a shoe-shop clerk enough to get him to shag her. Sitting on the edge of her bed, she noticed another text from Vivie, but she just couldn't face that now. She was about to slip into her nightshirt when she thought better of it and crawled in between the sheets naked. It felt lovely. It would have felt even lovelier if Finn had slid into bed next to her all hard and ready to play.

She could hear the shower running in the bathroom, and maliciously she hoped it was a cold one that had nothing to do with being dirty. She turned off the lamp on her night stand and rolled over on her side, still trying to get her head around the events of the past twenty-four hours.

And suddenly she wasn't alone. Suddenly the demon presence filled all the space beneath her skin and expanded beyond to wrap around her like silk. Once again she felt the full roundness of femininity wriggling close to her, nuzzling up to her, embracing her, and she couldn't hold back a moan at the feel of tight nipples against her spine and soft pubic curls nestling up to her bottom. It didn't matter that they weren't physical. They felt stunningly real, and powerfully arousing. The warm breath against her ear was sweet and comforting. 'Don't feel bad, darling,' a female voice purred inside her head. 'He's afraid, that's all. He's afraid I might damage you somehow.' A hand cupped her breast, a thumb raked her hardening nipple.

'Will you?' Jill spoke out loud almost before she realised it. 'Will you damage me?'

'Of course not, my sweet Jill. Your flesh is precious to me, more so than you know. I would never harm you. Never.'

'What do you want from me, Eleanor?' This time Jill was careful not to speak out loud. For the first time since he sidled up to her in the pub, she wasn't so anxious to draw Finn's attention. This was her chance for a little girl talk. Girl talk with a lust demon. Jesus, the insanity of her situation was astounding.

'All I want is to share your body, Jill. I've been around a long time. I've experienced so many things.' Jill felt the brush of warm lips against her nape. 'So very many things, and yet there've been long passages of time in which my consciousness has had no place to anchor. Oh, Jill, it's such an empty space, eternity, when there's no flesh in which to express consciousness.' Eleanor snuggled still closer and a hand that wasn't physically there moved down to rest against Jill's pubis. She quivered at the touch.

Eleanor continued. 'But you, my darling, have flesh, lovely, voluptuous, delicious flesh. And yet with it you've experienced so little. You fear the lust that partners flesh, what it longs for, what it's capable of, what boundaries it may move beyond. I feel the ache in you, the need. I felt it before I took you. That ache to experience what you've not been brave enough to allow is what drew me to you, what I felt when you stumbled into Finn's shop. You were like light shining into darkness. I could see nothing else. I wanted nothing else. But you.'

The embrace tightened and Jill found herself writhing against the mattress, grinding her bottom back against the demon femininity pressed next to her. It was then that she realised the hand she felt between her legs was not the imagined one but her own, fingers circling her clit and dipping in between the swell of her, still wet from the evening's heat, still vibrant with the scent of Finn. And for a second she resented him washing the olfactory evidence of their lovemaking down the drain, covering himself in the unnatural scent of soap and deodorant, when she wanted him to smell of her, when she wanted him to smell of them, super-heated and driven, in the throes of a hard animal fuck. She inhaled deeply the smell of him on her body, inside her body, and contemplated the way her scent wrapped around it, mixed through it, enhanced it, made it smell like it belonged there, closer to her than any other scent that wasn't her own. The imagined arms tightened around her and another warm kiss brushed her nape, feeling as real as anything she had ever felt. The circle and thrust, circle and thrust of her fingers intensified. She felt desperate for the release that was demanded by thoughts of the man now naked in her shower and by the fondling and cuddling of the demon woman whose caress, non-corporeal or not, felt urgent, insistent, needy.

'What do *you* want, Jill Hart? You can have it, you know. You're not Finn's prisoner. As long as I'm inside you, you'll never be anyone's prisoner. If you don't want to sleep, you don't have to.' She laughed softly. 'I'm not as stupid as Finn thinks. I know exactly what your body's capable of and what would most pleasure it, both things you would like very much to know. Isn't that so?'

Jill nodded her response into the darkness. Then the voice felt closer still. 'Get dressed, Jill. We're going out.'

'But what about Finn?'

'Nobody knows Finn better than I do, sweetie,' the voice came again. 'Trust me, I know how to give him the slip. In fact I know how to give him something even better than the slip.' She tsk-tsked. 'Of course I'm not going to hurt him, you silly goose. I would never hurt our Finn. I'll just give him a little something to think about. Go on now, get dressed. That's a good girl.'

* * *

Thirty minutes later they were dancing in Juno. Jill was wearing the skirt she'd borrowed from Vivie, a black vest that showed plenty of cleavage, and the fabulous boots. Her hair was down and the make-up was minimal. Clearly not from the same school of fashion as Vivie, Eleanor had assured her that, in her case, less was more.

Jill was dancing, something she would never have been brave enough to do without Vivie there to egg her on. Vivie, Eleanor, what was the difference, she wondered. She still wasn't brave enough to strike out on her own. 'Neither is Vivie,' Eleanor whispered. 'That's why she drags you along.'

And, in truth, this time was considerably different. Jill had danced with three different blokes since she'd arrived, and the one she was dancing with now looked like he might play rugby or something equally physical when he wasn't shaking his very nice booty on the dance floor.

'Mmmm,' Eleanor purred against her ear. 'He definitely fancies you, and I detect wood developing below deck.'

Jill wasn't sure if the improvement in her peripheral vision came from being demon-possessed or simply from the fact that she'd never needed to sneak a peek at a man's crotch before. But Eleanor wasn't wrong. The guy's fly was filling out very nicely indeed. The thought that Jill could be fucking him very shortly tightened her pussy in the tiny gusset of her thong, already damp with exciting possibilities. The knot in her stomach tightened in empathy at the thought of actually letting this bloke, this stranger, ride her. Before her encounter with Finn in Kinky Boots, she'd never even come close to picking up someone in a bar.

As the music changed to a slow beat, some song that Jill, with her total lack of interest in pop culture, didn't recognise, the man pulled her into his arms. He wasn't as big as Meinrad, but he was plenty big enough, and for a second she fought the urge to flee as strong arms closed around her and a hand settled low on her back just above the swell of her bottom.

'It's all right,' Eleanor assured her. 'He's OK.'

The man, whose name she didn't know, bent and brushed a kiss across her ear. 'You smell so good,' he said.

She smelled like Finn, she thought, and suddenly she felt guilty, which made her angry. She had no reason to feel guilty. She didn't belong to Finn. She was nothing to him, other than the duty he'd been saddled with because the demon he was supposed to be controlling got out of hand. She expected some tart remark from Eleanor at that thought, but the demon said nothing.

Before she could think too much about it, the man's mouth found hers in an awkward hunchback of a position that his added height required. The kiss was sloppy, too wet, too much tongue, too suffocating. He lacked Finn's finesse in the lip and mouth department. The fact that she was making comparisons made her even more angry, but she was too nervous to press the issue and take back control of the kiss. Instead, she managed to level a palm against his chest to give herself a little breathing space. He mistook her effort as mutual attraction and guided her hand inside the open top buttons of his shirt to rest against a sweaty pec. 'Come on,' he panted, 'let's get out of here.'

She balked, and fought back panic. 'I can't leave.' The sudden rush of nerves made her knees weak, made her feel like she might hyperventilate. 'I'm waiting for a friend. We said we'd meet here.'

'There you are, darling! I've been looking all over for you.' Finn pushed in between her and Rugby Man, who made no effort to stop him, but gave a little shrug and offered her a look that said she was a cock-tease. Then he moved to the side of the dance space and immediately began talking to a redhead with enormous tits.

'What the hell do you think you're doing?' Finn pulled her close, forcing the breath from her lungs. 'I leave you alone with her for five minutes, Eleanor, and you get her into trouble. You see, this is exactly why I don't trust you, why I keep you on a tight leash.'

'It's my fault,' Jill said. 'I couldn't sleep. I wanted to ... wait a minute.' She stepped back and placed her hands on her hips, jostling a couple dancing behind them. 'The last time I checked, I was an adult. I don't have to ask permission to do what I want, and I don't have to apologise for it.'

He reached for her, but she stepped back again. 'You left her alone.' It was Eleanor using her vocal cords, and the change was so swift and seamless that it startled both Jill and Finn.

'I didn't leave her alone.' He shook his head in confusion. 'I didn't leave you alone, Jill. I was right in the next room, I just wanted you to be safe.'

'Well, as you can see, I am safe, so you can go home and go back to sleep now. That is what you want, isn't it?'

'Fuck.' He spoke between barely parted lips. 'Is that what you think I want? You think I want to sleep? If I'd been able to sleep, I wouldn't have heard you leave, would I?'

'You heard us leave?' Jill yelled to be heard over the music. Another couple jostled her up against Finn, but she pushed back.

'Of course I heard you leave.' He jerked his head toward the bar. 'I've been standing there watching you. I don't mind you having a little fun, but when that arsehole moved in for the grope, that was enough.' Was she mistaken, or did she sense Eleanor was quite smug about Finn's behaviour? But then her anger took over.

'You followed me?'

'Hell, yes, I followed you. You can't really believe I'd let you out of my sight, can you?' Then he grabbed her by the shoulders and pulled her to him close and tight, taking her mouth in a brutal kiss that ended in a sharp bite. In a move that was startlingly swift he cupped her arse cheeks and pulled her tight against him. And Jesus, he was hard, and regardless of who might be watching, she practically climbed his body in an effort to get closer. Everything inside her sparked and the sounds Eleanor was making inside her head were positively copulatory as she ate Finn's mouth and rubbed against him. 'I want you so bad I can hardly stand it, Jill. Don't you know that?'

She was tempted to fuck him right there in Juno with the whole Saturday-night crowd looking on, but instead she pulled away, and it was as though she were suddenly an island in the middle of a vast ocean with a clear view all around her. 'No I don't know that, Finn. And we need to talk.' For the first time she wasn't sure who was doing the speaking, her or Eleanor, but it didn't matter. There were too many things that needed to be dealt with if she were going to survive being possessed by a lust demon. Finn ran a hand through his already mussed hair, squared his shoulders then led her off the dance floor.

* * *

They opted for neutral ground, an Indian restaurant whose name Jill forgot even before they were seated in a cramped corner near the back, the only place free in the late-night mishmash of clubbers and pubbers. Strangely she eschewed her usual biryani in favour of chicken jalfrezi. Even as the fiery dish burned her tongue and made her eyes water, she relished all the flavours she had never experienced before, but in the back of her mind she knew that Eleanor liked Indian spices, hot and steamy. Across from her, Finn picked at his korma.

He shifted uncomfortably in his seat. 'Why are we here?' he asked.

'Well, first of all, I'm hungry, and Eleanor was in the mood for a good curry. Secondly and most importantly, if you're going to be Eleanor's chaperone while she's in residence, Finn, then we need to set some ground rules.'

He raised an eyebrow, polished off his pint of

Kingfisher and motioned for the waiter to bring him another. 'Ground rules?'

She leaned across the table and hissed at him. 'I'm possessed, for chrissake, remember?'

He blinked.

'And I don't even know what that means. What little I do know is no thanks to you or your Sole Alliance mates. You ordered me home like a naughty child and sent me to bed.'

'Jesus, Jill.' He looked around as though he feared someone might be listening in, then leaned across so close that they nearly banged heads over the small table. 'I'm trying to keep you safe, not punish you.'

'I know that, really I do, but –' she spoke between barely parted lips '– Eleanor's a lust demon.'

He gave another quick glance around the room, then did his own version of talking without opening his mouth. 'I know what Eleanor is, Jill. That's the problem, isn't it?'

'No, that's not the problem,' she said. They paused politely while the waiter delivered Finn's pint, and when he went off to take the order at the table next to them she said, 'The problem is that a lust demon chose me to possess, Finn. That's the problem. She could have chosen anyone, and she chose me because ...'

'Because?' Finn said.

She fidgeted with her napkin, suddenly embarrassed

and shy. 'Because I'm inexperienced.' She hurried onward, fearing that he might laugh. 'But that doesn't mean I'm not filled with lust, Finn, with fantasies, with desires, powerful desires. That's why she possessed me.'

'I still don't see your point.'

'The point is I want what Eleanor's offering. I know that now. I want all that I've never had, all that I would never be brave enough to pursue without … well, without demon courage.' In her head she heard Eleanor giggle softly at her turn of phrase.

'So you want a fuck fest,' Finn said. His jaw was set hard, his shoulders were tight and block-square.

'I'm willing to be open about Eleanor's desires, and about my own.' She held his gaze. 'What I'm not willing is to be treated like I'm under house arrest. If you don't want to fuck me, that's fine. But I –'

'Wait a minute, who said I didn't want to fuck you? I'd think it was pretty obvious how badly I want to fuck you.'

The people at the table next to them gave a quick glance and half sniggered over their bottle of white wine. Finn hissed a whisper. 'If I were any harder, I'd be lifting the table off the floor.'

Jill choked on her water, and the couple next to them couldn't make their efforts to pretend not to be paying attention any more obvious.

When the coughing subsided, she took a deep breath

and spoke. 'Then why did you opt for a cold shower rather than my warm bed?'

'I thought that would be obvious too.' If Finn had leaned any further over the table he'd have been on top of it. 'I wanted to be sure it was you who wanted me and not Eleanor using you to get to me.'

'Oh, it's me all right, Finn. Eleanor may want you too, but I was there first without her, remember? And I promise you, there are things I want to do with you that don't involve raising the table.'

His eyelids fluttered and the groan that escaped his lips was nearly painful. 'Then why the hell are we here rather than at your place or mine?'

'Negotiations.' Again Jill wasn't sure if it were she or Eleanor who had spoken.

'Negotiations?'

'What I want out of lust-demon possession.'

'Jesus, you make it sound like a cruise or something,' he said.

She folded her arms across her chest and glared at him.

'All right!' He glared back. 'Fair enough. And it's safe to assume that what you want involves sex.'

She nodded enthusiastically. 'Lots of sex. Kinky sex, dirty, filthy, nasty sex, and I expect you to be more than just a chaperone and a gaoler.'

He raised an eyebrow and sat back in his chair as Eleanor took over the conversation.

'I want a body that's not a prison, Finn, and Jill's is so very much the body of my dreams. And I want her amply rewarded for her generosity. There's no need to play naïve with me, because we both know you're not. Between the two of us, we know exactly how to reward Jill for playing host to me, and I reckon that's the least we can do.' The chuckle that slipped up Jill's throat was wicked, and she felt it all the way down to her clit. 'Oh, don't tell me you don't want to play with us, Finn Masters, because I know better.' And almost, but not quite, before she knew what she was doing, Jill slid down into her seat just enough to place the sole of one sexy boot in between Finn's legs and press it solicitously up against the delightful strain of his erection through his jeans.

He held her gaze, his eyes suddenly storm-cloud dark as she had never seen them, dark, and somehow frightening in a way that went straight to her crotch. Then he scooted forward in his seat and uttered a soft grunt as he pressed up tight against her foot. 'Tell me what you want, Jill.' He reached under the table and stroked her calf just above the boot with a warm hand. 'Tell me what you want, and I'll see that you get it.'

# *Chapter 9*

'I want to be tied up.' Jesus! Where the hell had that come from? Was she out of her mind? She figured she could blame Eleanor. Didn't Finn say Eleanor would make sure her darkest desires were front and centre?

Finn held her gaze. For a long moment he said nothing, only studied her as though he were seeing her for the first time. 'You're sure?'

'Yes,' she said. 'Positive.' And she was, though until now, she wouldn't have known it.

Still holding her gaze, he fished his iPhone from his pocket.

'Meinrad, close up the shop and bring the ropes. My place.' He disconnected and turned his attention back to her. 'Meinrad has a lot more finesse with tying people up than I do.' Suddenly he didn't seem to care if the people next to them heard. 'If it were me, I'd just tie you to the bed with your knickers and shag you senseless.'

She was pretty sure that would have worked just fine

for her. In fact the picture it created in her head sent a new flood of lust to her panties.

Kinky Boots was just up the street, and Meinrad was closing up shop when Finn force-marched Jill past the door and around the back.

Inside the flat, Finn locked the door behind them and guided her through the kitchen and the lounge down a narrow hall past the bathroom. 'My bedroom,' he said, opening a door into a room that was unusually big for an apartment tucked behind a shop in Shoreditch. The room was an eclectic hodgepodge that was probably the perfect psychological study of Finn Masters. Any other time, Jill would have loved to take it all in, but right now she couldn't take her eyes off a very large brass bed that looked like it came straight from an American western movie. Both the headboard and the footboard were ornately twisted, finely worked brass.

He moved behind her and kissed her neck. 'The basement is rigged for suspension, but since you've never been tied before, we'll start with a nice comfy bed. Now –' he shifted his hips against her until she could feel his hard-on '– take off your clothes. All of them.'

She balked. 'And Meinrad is –'

'Is going to see you naked, yes, Jill. By the time he's done, he'll be very familiar with your body.' He nodded to her clothes. 'Now get undressed. This is what you want, isn't it?'

For a second, she had the strange urge to cry or to run. She did neither. She squared her shoulders and slipped the vest off over her head. As she unzipped the skirt and stepped out of it, he nodded to her boots. 'Leave those on.'

While she slipped out of her bra and knickers, Finn stood unmoving, watching her, his eyes unreadable, the erection in his jeans unmissable. When she was naked except for the boots, he gathered her clothing and laid it across the back of a black leather settee.

There was a soft knock on the door and Meinrad entered the room with several hanks of what looked like ordinary rope. He nodded his greeting to Finn, then his gaze came to rest on Jill, and she felt her entire body blush at his inspection. 'Turn around,' he said.

She obeyed.

He made some sound low in his throat that could have passed as either approval or not. Then he placed a large hand on her shoulder and turned her back to face him. She noticed he wore the Kinky Boots uniform T-shirt stretched tight across his very broad chest. The shop name was punctuated by the hard pressure of nipples on muscular pecs. The black jeans he wore rode low on his hips. The wave of lust that rushed over her was staggering. How had she not noticed how sexy he was?

Then Finn moved to stand beside him, and she understood. Even though Meinrad was by far the larger man,

Finn dominated the room. Finn dominated the space. Finn dominated every second of the last twenty-four hours of her life, as though he had shoved his way in and pushed everything else out. It did things to her, that thought, things that were way beyond lust, things that were a lot more frightening than being possessed by a demon. He stood gazing down at her from some neutral distance that made her feel very much alone, as though the world and everyone in it had receded, leaving her to await her fate. Eleanor was keeping a low profile.

Finn spoke without preamble. 'Unless something's hurting you, while Meinrad's binding you, you're not to speak. You're only to move when he moves you. You're to do exactly as he says. You're to accept what he does to you in total passivity. Is that clear?'

'Is he going to fuck me?' She was embarrassed the minute she said it but it was too late to take it back.

'If I want him to, yes,' Finn said.

If Finn wanted him to. Dear God, what was she doing? Suddenly she felt unsteady on her feet. She didn't know Meinrad. Not like she knew Finn. And yet the thought of the big man hammering her with his enormous cock while she was all trussed up was at least as exciting as it was uncomfortable. The thought that he would do so only at Finn's bidding excited her even more.

'There'll be no safe word,' Finn continued. 'All you have to do is tell Meinrad to stop. Or if at any time he thinks you're not fit to continue, he'll stop, and that'll be that. Are we clear?'

She nodded. 'And what about you?'

'Meinrad's acting on my behalf.' Finn held her in a cool gaze. 'He'll do as I say, and so will you, unless you choose at any point not to play.' For a long moment he studied her, as though he might see something, perhaps some flaw, perhaps some weakness, she didn't know what. He seemed too far away to tell. She held her breath. Waiting.

At last he blinked and stepped back, still holding her gaze. 'I'll ask you again, Jill. Are you sure this is what you want?'

She nodded, afraid to speak for fear her heart would jump out of her throat. Then she remembered to breathe again.

Finn said nothing. He took her hands in his and offered them to Meinrad, who took both her wrists in one huge palm and tied them across one another in a simple looped knot from which she could have easily escaped if she'd wanted. Then he led her to the bed and guided her onto it. There, he secured her hands to the headboard with several feet of slack, enough to allow him to work around her and at the same time allow Finn to observe from every angle. A quick glance over her shoulder revealed Finn had pulled a ladderback chair to the side of the bed and sat emotionlessly looking on. A quick glance was all she got before Meinrad settled her into a kneeling position facing the wall with her hands resting on the headboard.

In the beginning, it felt as though she were being decorated with rope; that's the best way Jill could describe what Meinrad was doing to her. The rope was softer than she expected it to be and not unpleasant against her bare skin. The embarrassment she felt came, flashed hot, then passed as Meinrad looped the rope and efficiently placed knots above her breasts and then below and then tightened and cinched his efforts until the harnessing effect squeezed and pinched and offered up each of her breasts in a tight little nest of rope, like ripe fruit topped by the cherry-hard rise of her nipples. She'd always had sensitive breasts and to have them so handled and bound made her whole chest burn with a need that was replicated in her pussy.

Meinrad worked in complete silence, his hands moving over her body as though she were nothing more than the canvas for what he was creating. His touch was exacting and his rhythm as he worked was hypnotic. Early on she realised that one of his hands was on her at all times. She remembered basic knot training from her childhood days in the Girl Guides. Right over left and under and through. Left over right and under and through. Rope threaded through competent fingers, rope slid over bare skin, coiling, twisting, binding, descending right over left and left over right, pressing a column of knots down the length of her spine before looping around her waist and embracing her belly. Again. And again.

Yes, she was his canvas, and what he created took its shape against her flesh, but his art didn't happen without exacting a price from him, and in her peripheral vision, as he reached around her to secure a knot over her navel, she caught a glimpse of the erection set tight in his black jeans, and she felt the hitch of his breathing not quite hidden in the rhythm of right over left, left over right. As he crossed the ropes around her body, she felt the heat of his breath whisper along her back next to the weaving and twisting and soft swishing of the rope along her spine.

With a tug of the rope every pore of her body responded to the tightening just as he nestled a knot against the pucker of her bottom and her gasp sounded like a rush of wind in the stretching silence. Meinrad gave a little pull and her clit hardened in empathy with the pressure between her buttocks.. Then without warning, he slipped an arm around her and turned her over as he pulled two strands of rope up between her legs, up tight against her upper thighs like the elastic of knickers, or a tightly cinched climber's harness. That done, with a deft movement of his fingers he secured a knot just over her clit, and this time she cried out in the strange mix of discomfort and arousal. The whole gape of her was pressed between the two strands of rope, knotted at fore and aft like a ship, narrow and thick-hulled.

There was barely time to get used to the strange rub and pressure between her legs, or the knot that felt like the tip of a thick finger attempting to breach her bottom, before Meinrad began to bind her thighs to her lower legs and ankles, making the position in which she knelt mandatory. With each knot, with each looping of the rope, he forced her bent legs further apart until she was wide open, yet at the same time held closed by the ropes between her legs. Bound and kneeling on the bed, she tried to breathe deeply, tried to fight back the panic of her own helplessness, something she had never experienced before. She was dangerously close to hyperventilating, and Eleanor seemed to be completely absent from the whole event.

'Shall I continue?' Meinrad asked.

She nodded, swallowing the panic back down against the hammering of her heart that seemed to fill the whole inside of her from the space where her brain was supposed to be all the way down to her trussed up pussy.

'Then you have to relax,' he said. 'Breathe slowly and deeply. And trust me. Can you do that?'

She glanced at Finn who gave the tiniest nod of his head, and she closed her eyes, took a deep breath and nodded her consent.

'Good girl,' Meinrad whispered. Then he untied her wrists with a single slip of a knot. She barely had time to feel the rope slide away before Finn joined Meinrad.

Each man took one of her arms and bound it to the brasswork of the headboard. They began their efforts just below her arm pits and worked their way down to her wrists, the ropes like two snakes coiling away from her. Right over left and under and through. Left over right and under and through, until at last her arms were as spread and as open as her legs, bound across the headboard as though she were about to be crucified.

She closed her eyes, fighting back panic again, fighting back tears, fighting back an avalanche of emotions she hadn't expected. She had let two men she barely knew bind her until she was totally helpless. They said they'd release her. They said all she had to do was ask. So why the hell wouldn't she ask? What kind of people enjoyed tying up an innocent woman? What kind of neurotic nutter would willingly let herself be tied up, even ask for it? As she struggled to breathe, the tears came unbidden. She couldn't wipe them away. She couldn't hide them. She was powerless, and being naked was nothing compared to whatever else was laid bare, whatever it was that made her weep like a stupid child. There was no sign of Eleanor, who'd promised her she'd never be a prisoner as long as she resided inside her. Well, how much more of a prisoner could she be? And how could it be that somewhere in the mix of panic and anger and frustration and fear, and so many other feelings she couldn't sort out, her body still buzzed with arousal?

'Shshsh!'

Her eyes fluttered open just as Finn planted a kiss on her lips. 'It's all right, Jill. You're all right.' He motioned to Meinrad who brought him a mirror that reminded Jill of the kind used at hairdressers.

'Leave us,' Finn said without looking away from her. Meinrad turned silently and left the room.

'Look at you,' Finn said, holding the mirror first to her tear-streaked face, then to the incredible bulge of her breasts and nipples, which he cupped and caressed. He placed a kiss upon each one before he moved the mirror down between her legs. 'Look how beautiful you are.' With the hand not holding the mirror he pressed gently on the knot resting against her clit and she whimpered and jerked against her bonds. Then he moved a finger with a feather touch down where she was pressed between the two strands of rope. Without warning, he pushed two fingers into her restrained cleft, and the sound that came from her throat was primal, angry, full of need.

But Finn kept stroking and probing. She could feel herself slickening and swelling around his fingers, and she struggled to move against him to get the stimulation she needed. But the shifting of her hips only tightened the knots against her. She could see all of it, every press and grind and quiver, in the mirror Finn held between her legs. Before she could struggle further, he lay the mirror aside and placed a restraining hand on the flat of her belly. 'Hold still, Jill. Just hold still and let me do it.' Still probing and scissoring her slit with two fingers, he opened his fly, and she watched as he manoeuvred his arching erection free.

'I'm going to fuck you now, Jill, because I've waited long enough. And you're going to hold still while I do it, while I make you come. Then I'm going to fill your little trussed-up pussy until you can't hold any more because that's how full I am for you.' He pulled off his jeans and positioned himself between her bound legs, where he lifted and manoeuvred her until she was practically on his lap, while she held her breath in anticipation. God, he couldn't possibly need it more than she did.

At last he rose up onto his haunches and pushed into her, until she supported all of her weight on her bound arms and on his body. The grimace on his face, the growl in his throat, the way he caught his breath could have been little different if he had just been run through with a knife. The fit of him inside her, which was always tight, was made still tighter by the bind of the ropes. The pressure his body exerted drove the knots into her clit and her backside in an exquisite cocktail of pain and pleasure and simulation of raw nerve endings that she had never experienced before and wasn't sure she would survive to experience again. How could anything be so uncomfortable and so exquisite at the same time?

With the second thrust, he rose up onto his knees and

ripped his T-shirt off over his head so that his bare chest rubbed against her bulging breasts in rhythm to the tug and press of the knots. Then he cupped her bottom and impaled her still deeper. She could neither bear down nor press up to meet him, bound as she was. He wasn't being gentle, nor did she want him to be. At the moment, she wanted him to rip her apart if that's what it took to scratch the itch that threatened to drive her totally insane.

'I think I'm gonna die,' she gasped.

'Not before you come,' he grunted. 'Not before we both come.'

And she did. She came in an exquisite convulsion of pain and pleasure. His orgasm spilled into her like a tidal wave, the weight of it hammering her insides even as the weight of his body abraded her tender flesh beneath the caress of the ropes.

She was still crying and trembling as he unbound her with efficient efforts that took far less time than she would have imagined. When she was free, and her limbs tingled with the returning ability to move, he took off her boots and rubbed her legs vigorously.

Then he lifted her into his arms and carried her into the bathroom. Someone had drawn a warm bath fragrant with lavender and other herbs she didn't recognise, all making mountains of foam in an enormous roll-top tub. He settled her into the suds and, with a soft sponge, gently began to wash the tender places that bore the red marks of the ropes. And still she cried like she'd never stop. He said nothing, only silently, carefully tended her. At last, when he had done all he could do, he disappeared and returned with a sandwich and a bottle of cold water, which she drank down thirstily. Then he fed her until she had eaten her fill and the sobbing had subsided.

That done, he climbed into the bathtub behind her, pulled her in between his thighs and pillowed her head against his chest, where she dozed close to the beating of his heart. When she came back to herself, he was helping her out of the tub and drying her with a thick terry towel. He carried her to his bed, tucked her in, settled in next to her and pulled her close.

'Are you all right?' he whispered.

It was then she realised that inside her Eleanor was blissful. She nodded her reply, barely able to hold her eyes open. 'It was what I wanted.' There was a long stretch of silence, but she could almost feel him looking at her in the darkness.

'You're not sorry?' he asked.

Eleanor's bliss was expansive, or maybe it wasn't all Eleanor's bliss. Hadn't she read somewhere that cathartic experiences could become ecstatic? It was too much to think about now. She sighed. 'No. No, I'm not sorry, Finn. I'm not sorry at all. I just never imagined it would make me feel … like this.'

# *Chapter 10*

'There. You see, that wasn't so bad, was it? In fact it was delicious, for her and for me.'

'You were fairly subtle,' Finn said. 'That was a surprise.'

Instantly Jill knew she was dreaming, and yet it felt as though she were eavesdropping. She was sitting in the ladderback chair next to Finn's bed. No, she was actually tied to the ladderback chair with dozens of elegant knots. From her bound position she watched herself, elbow bent, head resting on one hand, looking down at Finn who lay next to her. Of course it wasn't her, was it? It was Eleanor. That was obvious to her from her position of observation in the dream world.

'It was Jill's fantasy, remember? And I get the most out of her body when I let her control the experience.' Eleanor offered Finn a little pout. 'Meinrad must have been terribly disappointed that, after all his efforts to bind her so beautifully, you didn't allow him to fuck her.' She lay back on the pillow, one hand stroking her erect nipple above the duvet. 'Still, I suppose he'll get his chance. She'll want to fuck him, you know?'

'Maybe not,' Finn said.

'She isn't as fragile as you think. She would have been fine to shag Meinrad. She was in such a state, Meinrad would have only enhanced what she was feeling.'

'It was my call to make, Eleanor, so just drop it.' Finn shoved the duvet back and sat up on the edge of the bed, and Jill admired the straight lines of his back, ending in the muscular swell of his buttocks half hidden by the mattress and duvet.

Eleanor ran a finger down the length of his spine to linger at the crack of his arse, just exactly as Jill would have done if she had been lying there next to him. 'I think you're jealous. I think that's why you wouldn't let Meinrad fuck her. The same reason you wouldn't let that bloke at Juno fuck her. You don't want anyone else inside her, do you?'

'That's ridiculous, Eleanor. I just want her to be safe, and thanks to you, I can't guarantee that, can I?'

'Oh, Finn, why do you worry so?'

'You know why I worry.'

Eleanor pushed off the duvet and rose to kneel behind him to run hands along his shoulders and place a kiss against the spot where his pulse thudded in his neck. Then she brushed his wild morning hair away from his ear and spoke in what was barely a whisper, spoke so softly that Jill strained against her bindings to hear. 'That was a long time ago, Finn. It was a mistake. I never intended to hurt Lisa. You know that. It won't happen again, and certainly not with Jill. She's so much stronger, so much more herself. And so totally delightful, don't you think? Finn, I won't hurt her. I would never.'

'You said that about Lisa.' Finn shrugged off her embrace, and stood. 'And I was left to pick up the pieces.' Then he turned his back on her and left the bedroom, slamming the door behind him.

\* \* \*

Jill woke with a start, sitting upright in the honeyed threads of sunlight that penetrated the high window of Finn's room. She was alone in the big bed, and the sound of traffic on Shoreditch High Street was all that broke the silence. She chafed her arms and looked around at framed vintage playbills of Gilbert & Sullivan productions next to brightly coloured posters of comic books displayed in brightly coloured frames. Built-in bookshelves along one wall overflowed. The black leather settee was still draped in her clothes. The shelves, the bedside table, the windowsill were all littered with erotic sculptures ranging from tiny all the way up to a free-standing statue of Priapus at the end of the settee, enormous cock hefted at the ready. The ropes were gone but the room still smelled of last night's sexual escapades. Beneath that was the smell of herbs that made her think of a summer field, and beneath that still was the scent of maleness, the scent of Finn, and it was that scent that she felt low in her belly and wet between her thighs.

'He's working.' Eleanor's voice filled Jill's head, and Jill let out a startled gasp. It was still not something she was used to, being demon-possessed. 'Finn. He's working. He only left a little while ago.'

The dream came back to Jill, and she shivered. But before she could dwell on it, Eleanor's presence settled like a warm blanket around her, and she couldn't quite remember what it was from the dream that had frightened her. Anyway it was just a dream, wasn't it? 'He's working on a Sunday?' she asked.

'Not in Kinky Boots. He has other responsibilities, Sole Alliance responsibilities.'

'I thought you were Sole Alliance's responsibility.' Jill said.

'Responsibility isn't exactly the word I would have used,' Eleanor huffed. 'But if you choose to view me that way, well, let's just say I'm not their only responsibility.'

Jill lay back on the bed and stretched against the sheets that Finn dreamed on. She wondered if he dreamed about her. For a moment she basked in the strange afterglow until curiosity got the best of her, then she threw back the covers and moved cautiously to stand in front of the mirror over the dresser. The ache of a lot of sex after a long abstinence was all over her. It was an ache that made her smile. As the night's adventures came rushing back to her in detail, she examined her body. There were places where the ropes had left marks, but on a whole very few, and in spite of herself Jill felt disappointed not to have more.

'Meinrad's very good at what he does.' Eleanor said. 'If you wanted to be marked, you only needed to ask.'

'I'll remember that next time.' And to her surprise, Jill found she wasn't totally opposed to the idea of a next time. She tilted her head from side to side, cupping her breasts, studying herself. 'I don't look any different,' she said. 'I mean, I figured being possessed and all, I might look a little different, I don't know, different colour eyes or something.'

Eleanor laughed softly. 'It doesn't work that way, my sweet Jill. But trust me, though you may not look different from your point of view, from mine there's suddenly a great deal more to you. As though you've decided to open up a few more rooms in the mansion. And other people will notice the difference, though they may not be able to put their finger on it.'

\* \* \*

Jill didn't linger at Finn's place, in spite of the desire to learn more about him. For some reason she had an overwhelming urge to go home. Eleanor assured her that it was normal to seek out the familiar when so much of her context had changed in such a short time. She threw on Vivie's well-worn skirt and headed back to her house, stopping at the Co-op on the way to buy the ingredients for a fry-up. She was starving.

At home, she showered and dressed. The search through her closet revealed the basic elements for a bolder, sexier look. The urge had always been there. She'd just not been brave enough for bold or sexy until now. She chose a short flip skirt that was candy-apple red and an oversized white silk shirt barely buttoned over the plunge of an ivory lace bra.

After a feast Eleanor enjoyed as much as she did, she made a backup of the recording of her boss from the BlackBerry and drafted a letter to Human Resources, with Eleanor adding her advice as she felt the need. She was just about to answer yet another text from Vivie when there was a knock on her door.

'That will be Finn,' Eleanor said. 'He's worried about you, and he's horny as hell.'

Jill nearly dropped her BlackBerry before she threw it onto the coffee table. On her way to the door, she undid another button on her blouse.

Eleanor giggled. 'I don't think seduction will be necessary, hon.'

From the open door, Finn glared at her, arms folded across his chest. 'You could have at least left me a message,' he said. 'I was worried.' She smiled to herself as his gaze dipped instinctively to the barely buttoned front of her shirt.

'I couldn't find a pen,' she replied, motioning him in and shutting the door behind him. 'And I didn't have your mobile number. I figured you'd guess I went home. I needed a shower and some clean clothes.'

He grabbed her by the lapels of her shirt and pulled her up onto her toes and into a deep hungry kiss. 'You can't just go off without telling me,' he said when he put her back on her feet. 'I know you and Eleanor are best mates at the moment, but you've got to trust me, she's unpredictable, and she's not vulnerable to the hazards of humanity like you are.'

'You mean like being tied to a bed and having my brains fucked out, those kinds of hazards?'

When he didn't smile, she shook his shoulders gently. 'I'm joking, Finn, just joking. Last night was amazing, really. I'm still trying to get my head around it but otherwise –'

'I need you, Jill. I need you bad.' He grabbed her by the wrist and guided her hand to rest against his fly and she caught her breath.

'Jesus, Finn, how did you even get up the stairs?'

'I was motivated.' He rubbed her hand against his crotch. 'Very motivated.'

'I don't have any ropes,' she said.

He held her gaze. 'I told you I'll use your panties if I want to tie you up.'

'Fuck,' she whispered.

'Does it make you hot thinking about alternative uses I might find for your underwear? Shall I find out?'

With one hand he grabbed her by the lapel of her shirt and pulled her to him while the other scrunched and worried the hem of her skirt on the way to bare skin. Then he wriggled the crotch of her knickers aside and pushed into her with an upward thrust of two fingers. She practically came off the floor at the sudden but not unwelcome invasion.

'I was right,' he said, holding her gaze. 'Are you ever not ready for sex, Jill Hart?' He pulled his hand away and licked his fingers. 'First I want to eat you, then I want to fuck you until you can't stand up.'

She took his hand and led him to the over-stuffed chair crowded next to the sofa. At first she thought it might have been Eleanor instructing her, but it felt more like instinct as she stepped out of her panties and sat on the chair with her legs wide apart.

As she scrunched up her skirt, he stood watching, his fist rubbing up and down against the bulge in his jeans. She took her time, she didn't rush, in spite of the tingling need that snaked up between her legs, the muscle memory of her sex that made the anticipation of another orgasm at Finn's hands almost unbearable. When he groaned and cursed under his breath, she knew he could see her heavy need. Then she shifted her hips so he could see her whole cleft. With two fingers she spread herself, then dipped and swirled in and out of her pout while she thumbed her clit.

Finn dropped to his knees and pushed her open. The muscles that joined hips to thighs protested slightly after being tied up last night. 'You sore?' he asked, when she winced slightly.

'Not too sore for what you have in mind,' she replied.

He lifted her bare feet onto his shoulders and dived face-deep into the swell of her, tonguing his way up the smooth path of her perineum, parting her and dipping deep into her. The wet sounds of arousal accompanied the duet of their heavy breathing, and gasps of pleasure punctuated the Sunday morning quiet of her lounge. Licking and laving, he worked his way up until his pursed lips encircled her clit and he suckled and licked alternately. She held him against her, fingers curled tight in his hair, shifting and undulating against the delicious efforts of his tongue.

Over her heavy breathing she heard the zip of his fly and felt him fumble to release himself without missing a beat, licking and suckling, licking and suckling.

'Jill, I need you now,' he said, pulling her onto the floor. In her peripheral vision she caught a glimpse of his erection before he gathered her to him and impaled her. 'I'm too far gone to wait any longer,' he said with a hard thrust.

It didn't take long this time. A few thrusts and they were both over the edge. She thought he'd never stop coming. She wondered how they could be so fucking needy after last night.

For a long time, they lay on the floor in each other's arms catching their breath, her on top of him. He stroked her back gently, occasionally cupping and caressing her bottom, and when his breathing was slow and relaxed again, he spoke. 'What do you want next, Jill? You've been tied up, and my impression is that you weren't disappointed, so what next?'

His question surprised her. She wasn't entirely sure there would be more after last night. She had a strong sense that the experience had shaken him as much as it had her, and yet her answer was almost immediate. 'I want to watch.'

He blinked. 'You want to watch what? Two people fucking? An orgy? A threesome? What, Jill?'

'I want to watch you.'

'Me?' He pushed out from under her, breaking the physical connection in a flood of warmth. Then he pulled himself to a sitting position and ran a hand through his hair. 'You want to watch me do what?'

She shrugged. 'I don't know. What did you do, who did you do before you did me? You did have sex before I came into the picture, didn't you?'

'Yes, but …'

She laid a hand on his thigh, wet and sticky from his orgasm, and his penis responded with a jerk. 'Finn, when you breathe it's sexy. I've never met anyone who is more of a sexual being than you are, and it makes me hot to think about how you satisfy that need.'

He laid a hand on his returning erection and offered her a wicked smile. 'You want to watch me wank?'

'That's not exactly what I had in mind. Maybe some other time. What about Chelsea, do you have sex with Chelsea? She's quite hot, by the way. If I were you, I'd do her.'

He held her gaze as though he feared what she might do next. 'Sometimes, yes, when we're both horny and we end up together.'

'Thought so. And who else? Who else do you fuck, Finn?'

'Some of the other members of Sole Alliance, when they're here. We're all willing to help each other out if we need it.'

'Anyone outside Sole Alliance?'

'Not until you came along. It's safer that way.'

'It's dangerous to fuck people who aren't witches or magically endowed or whatever you all are?'

He raised an eyebrow. 'You ended up possessed by a demon.'

'Good point.' She still hadn't figured the downside to

that, in spite of all the warnings. 'What about Meinrad?' She said. 'Do you ever fuck him?'

His face reddened, and the muscles along his neck corded then relaxed. 'Sometimes, yes.'

The thought of the two men naked and sweating, muscles straining, seeking out masculine relief nearly sent her over the edge again. She caught her breath and laid a hand against her chest. 'Then I want to watch you with him.'

He cursed under his breath and worried his bottom lip with his teeth. 'This is what you want, not what Eleanor wants?'

'Oh, please.' Eleanor spoke through Jill's lips. 'I've seen you two humping each other's brains out ad nauseam, Finn. Give me a little credit for originality.'

Finn clenched his jaw, and made no attempt to disguise the irritation in his voice. 'If the two of us humping each other's brains out is not original enough for you, Eleanor, then why don't you suggest something else to Jill?'

'It's what I want,' Jill said, taking back her voice, and internally giving Eleanor the finger. 'Whether it's original or not.'

Eleanor, wherever she was inside Jill, was instantly contrite and silent. Jill continued. 'When you're making love to me, Finn, I'm too in the moment, too into you to really see you.'

For whatever reason, that statement elicited a sense of discomfort from Eleanor's quarter.

Finn studied her for a long moment, looking as though he'd half like to cut and run. Then he spoke. 'Why Meinrad?'

'Because he's been intimate with both of us. Last night you said that by the time we were finished, he'd be familiar with my body, and clearly he's familiar with yours. It just feels right.'

For another long moment he held her gaze, almost as though he expected her to change her mind. When she didn't he gave a curt nod. 'All right. If that's what you want, I'll see if I can arrange it with Meinrad. Now I'm going to take a shower.'

She watched his exquisite backside disappear down the hall toward the bathroom. She hoped she hadn't made him angry.

'Stop worrying,' Eleanor said. 'He's fine with shagging Meinrad. He's fine with being watched while he shags Meinrad. He's just not too confident in his way around you yet, and he doesn't want to disappoint you.'

Once she heard the shower running, she dressed and had just made herself a cup of tea when there was a loud knock on the door, the turning of a key in the lock, and Vivie burst in, practically throwing herself into Jill's arms. In typical Vivie fashion, she was already in mid-sentence. 'Oh, Jilly, thank God you're all right! I was so worried when you didn't answer my texts. I had visions of you dead on the floor, and it all being my fault, all my fault!'

Her embrace became a bear hug threatening to break ribs. 'My fault because I gave some friend of Alex's your name. Alex is the bloke I met at the Bluu Bar the other night. You remember? Well, he has a friend who said she has a friend who fancies you, and I was so excited for you that I didn't think. I gave him your name. But I didn't give him your number. I wouldn't do that. But then I got thinking with your name, he could find you easily enough. And then I didn't hear from you, and ...'

Her words died in her throat and she stepped away from Jill, giving a couple of gasps and nodding towards where Finn stood dripping on the floor, wrapped in a towel that barely covered the goodies.

'I ... left my bag in the lounge,' he managed before Vivie squared her shoulders, gave Jill a 'well done, you' nudge in the ribs with her elbow, then offered Finn her hand.

'I'm Vivie,' she said, 'and you must be Finn, the one who was desperately looking for my friend Jill.' Her eyes dipped to his towel. 'And I'd say you found her.'

'Yes, I found her all right,' he said. He grabbed his rucksack, then he paused before he headed back to the bathroom. He turned back, pulled Jill into his arms and gave her a toe-curling kiss, nearly losing his towel in the process.

As the two watched Finn's barely covered backside disappear down the hall, Vivie grabbed Jill by the arm and dragged her toward the sofa. 'Details, hon, I want details.' She helped herself to a sip of Jill's tea and sat down with a little wriggle of her bottom.

Somewhere in the vast undefined space inside her, Jill could feel Eleanor perched at full attention, just as anxious for a little nasty girl talk as Vivie was. Jill settled in to pick and choose what juicy bits were fit for the ears of the non-possessed.

# Chapter 11

'He's hot, Finn is.' Vivie was practically bouncing off her chair. 'Oh Jilly, I'm so excited for you!'

Jill couldn't prevent herself smiling when she thought about what Finn had done to her just before Vivie showed up. He'd left her flat, promising to be back in the evening after he'd finished his errands for Sole Alliance. Jill was already anticipating their reunion. Though Eleanor seemed to have enjoyed the girl talk over burgers and chips in the noisy, quirky bustle of the Breakfast Club, Jill still wasn't sure if she could trust her not to add her bit to the conversation at the most inopportune moment. From the Breakfast Club, they'd migrated around the corner to the Bluu Bar to share a bottle of wine and continue the conversation in a quieter place.

Jill was more than a little surprised by the glances of appreciation she drew from several men at the bar. She figured that was Eleanor's doing, since the last time she was in the Bluu Bar she had been all but invisible

114

to the opposite sex. She forced her attention back to Vivie, who was studying her like she was the menu at a five-star restaurant. One of those written in French. 'What?' she said.

Vivie leaned an elbow on the table and smiled at her friend. 'It's just, well, wow! You seem so different, so confident. You shag a sex god in a shoe shop on a Friday night. On Saturday morning you tell your boss to fuck himself, then quit your job. And on Sunday I show up to discover you've just been going at it with said sex god on the floor of your lounge. And all in one weekend. Still waters run deep.' Vivie lifted her glass in a toast.

She didn't know the half of it, Jill thought. They sipped their wine, and Vivie continued to study her in the afternoon sunlight streaming through the window. Jill pretended not to notice. 'I just can't get over how different you seem,' Vivie said. 'Stunning, actually.'

Inside whatever place demons hole up when they possess someone, Eleanor offered a smug 'I told you so'.

Jill couldn't remember a time when Vivie hadn't tried to change her into a darker, taller, more rounded version of her own model-perfect self. She had cajoled and brow-beaten her into having free make-overs at every cosmetic counter in every department store in the Greater London area. For Jill's last birthday, she had even given her a session with a wardrobe consultant, but to no avail. And now here they sat with Vivie looking on in admiration. What a difference a demon makes.

'I love the boots by the way,' Vivie said.

Jill had had another shower and was dressed in tight black jeans and a revealing vest just a few shades darker than the boots, a vest she only wore in the privacy of her flat. Until now. 'I still haven't paid for them,' she said with a quirk of a smile.

'You minx.' Vivie giggled. 'I just can't imagine you doing the nasty with Finn in his shoe store. That's so not you, Jilly.'

She had no idea, Jill thought.

Inside her head, Eleanor refused to take all the credit. After all, she reminded Jill, she hadn't actually been in residence for any of the foreplay in Kinky Boots.

They were on their second glass of wine, sitting on the high chairs at a chunky wooden table across from the bar. Vivie leaned closer. 'I'm not the only one totally awed by your very sexy self,' she said. 'You seem to be drawing the attention of that bloke in the corner.' Vivie gave a not-so-discreet sideways glance. 'The big one that looks like he could crush a lorry with one hand.' She gave him the once-over. 'Very nice. I like big men, I but definitely wouldn't want him on top.'

Jill felt her shoulders tighten. She didn't even have to look. Inside her head, Eleanor said. 'It's Meinrad all right. It must be his turn to keep an eye on us.'

Meinrad was making no effort to be stealthy. He was in his usual uniform of low-rider jeans and a black T-shirt that looked like it had been painted across his muscular chest. She thought about her dream, about Finn and Eleanor and the possibility of the big man ploughing her. 'On top's not the only way.' The words slipped out before she could stop them, and Vivie nearly sprayed her mouthful of wine across the table.

'Jill Hart, you naughty, naughty girl.' She leaned in conspiratorially close. 'Do you know him?'

'We've met, yes. He also works at Kinky Boots.'

'Fucking hell,' Vivie whispered, 'I'm shopping at the wrong shoe store.' She scooted her chair closer to Jill's, then shot Meinrad a very blatant stare. 'What do you reckon? Is he … you know … big all over?'

'Oh, he's big all right.' Jill wondered if Eleanor had suddenly turned off the internal editor. But in her mind's eye Eleanor raised innocent hands, refusing to take the blame.

Before Vivie could interrogate her further, Jill motioned Meinrad over. The look of embarrassment at being caught in the act was fleeting, or maybe only imagined. Meinrad wasn't known for great displays of emotion. But it still gave Jill a tingle of satisfaction forcing him to come clean. Before he could sit down, she said, 'Finn sent you.' It wasn't a question.

He nodded and, without so much as a greeting, took

the chair next to her, but not before she had the chance to notice he was at half-mast. The little gasp that escaped Vivie's lips told her she had noticed too. Jill wondered if he was always at half-mast and rising. 'You were talking about me,' he said, setting his lime and soda on the table.

'Vivie couldn't help noticing you staring at me, and the conversation went from there.' Jill said. 'She wondered if your cock was proportional. I said that it was.' Vivie blushed hard and mumbled something to her that she suspected wasn't very nice. Jill's intention had been to put Meinrad in his place, but she wondered if her wicked sense of satisfaction at turning the tables and embarrassing her friend as well was hers or Eleanor's.

Vivie forced a smile in Meinrad's direction.

Meinrad gave a peripheral glance at his lap and shrugged. For all his reaction she might have just told him that she liked his shirt.

'So,' Vivie said, trying to put the conversation back on track. 'You know Jill through Kinky Boots.'

'You could say that, I suppose,' Meinrad said, playing with the straw in his drink. 'I tied her up over there last night.'

Jill kicked him under the table, but he didn't seem to notice.

Vivie giggled nervously. 'For what? Stealing the boots?'

'Oh, no, she can have the boots. They're perfect for her. I tied her up so Finn could fuck her.'

This time he did flinch when Jill kicked him. But only a little.

Whatever was next on the polite conversation agenda died on Vivie's pursed lips. For a second she looked from one of them to the other, then she offered a low chuckle. 'Oh, I get it, and that's how she knows about your ...' She gave a little nod down to his lap.

'No. She knows about my cock because she saw me wa–'

'Jesus, Meinrad, shut up!' Jill kicked him hard this time and he still offered her nothing more than a cool gaze.

'You started it,' he said. 'I just assumed it was honesty time. By the way, Finn told me what you want us to do.'

Vivie practically buzzed with anticipation, leaning in for the latest. 'What do you want them to do, Jilly?' she said. 'Tell me.'

Before Jill could respond, Meinrad continued. 'I'm OK with it, of course.' He held her in a meaningful gaze. 'Finn and I both agreed that you're calling the shots, just like the other night, so of course we'll do whatever you want.'

Inside her head, Eleanor giggled, and Jill mentally flipped her the finger.

'Come on, Jilly, what shots are you calling? I'm dying to hear. I need details.' Vivie could barely remain in her seat. 'What the hell's going on? And how did I miss out?'

Thankfully, Vivie's Alex saved the day, showing up just in time to drag Vivie away to a jazz concert at some pub in Soho, but not before Vivie swore that, when she got back, she'd rack Jill and torture the details out of her if she didn't come clean.

'I believe she'd do it too,' Meinrad said, watching the couple leave. 'Though I doubt she could rack you as well as I could.' Jill wasn't sure Meinrad was coming on to her, or if he was just having a serious hard-on at the thought of getting to rack someone. He gave no indication one way or the other.

'You did that on purpose,' she hissed at him, nodding to where Vivie and Alex had just disappeared out the door.

'I did, yes. You deserved it.'

'I'm not the one who was spying,' Jill said.

'I'm not spying,' he replied. 'You knew I was there and you know why. Now finish your wine and I'll take you home.'

It was early evening when Meinrad walked Jill back to her flat. Inside, the big man settled on the sofa and took up the TV remote. 'You're tired,' he said. 'Get some rest. Finn will be back in a while.'

She was about to protest that he was being bossy to her in her own home, but then she realised he was right. She really was tired.

Before she headed off to her room, she turned to him. 'Thanks for last night. I didn't get a chance to tell you. What you did was amazing. The whole experience was amazing.'

The grunt of a response could have meant "you're welcome" or it could have meant "fuck off". With Meinrad it was always hard to tell.

As she headed for her room, Eleanor spoke quietly in her ear. 'Not surprising at all that you're tired after the past two days, sweetie. And you have no idea what a pleasure sleep and rest are after all these years without any. It all gets so boring. You just rest now. I'm sure Finn will wake you up when he gets in.' Her voice felt like a kiss against Jill's ear. 'If he doesn't I will.'

* * *

Jill didn't actually remember falling asleep, nor could she be certain what woke her up. Her first reminder of Eleanor's constant presence was a warm, slightly full feeling inside her abdomen, followed almost immediately by a growing tightness beneath the hood of her clit. If this was Eleanor's version of a wake-up call, she thought she could probably get used to it. But before she could manage to get a hand between her legs to answer that call, she heard shuffling followed by a grunt coming from the living room. Just as she was about to call out Finn's name, Eleanor mentally shushed her. 'Don't talk. Just go have a peek.'

There was another grunt, followed by what sounded like soft, slightly nervous male laughter, and Jill's pulse somersaulted in her throat. She had stripped completely to nap, something totally out of character for her, but she was getting used to being out of character. She fumbled in the dark for the nearest clothing, the flip skirt and the silk blouse. It was dark outside, but the moon was still close enough to full that the ambient light made it easy to see where she was going. Amber-coloured fallout from the lamplight in the lounge spilled into the hall. The tension in her belly, and below, and the exquisite tightening in her nipples made her suspect that some of her anticipation was Eleanor's. She tiptoed to the end of the hall, holding her breath. There she froze, as though she had been turned to stone.

On the sofa, Finn was just settling an open-mouthed kiss onto Meinrad's responsive lips. The sight was enough to make Jill's knees weak. Finn pulled away to tug the T-shirt off over the big man's massive shoulders, and his chest heaved into view. His heavily muscled pecs were topped with tight pink nipples, nipples that Finn ran his tongue around before he nipped and kissed his way down to Meinrad's navel, which peeked above the low ride of his jeans.

The view made every part of Jill's body buzz with excitement. She suspected that Eleanor had revved up the tension in some crazy demonic way. She had never felt so turned on. As Finn opened Meinrad's jeans and the man lifted his bum to allow them and his black boxers to be slid down over his thighs, Jill wriggled fingers up under her skirt.

'Don't do that,' Eleanor whispered. 'Keep your hands away from yourself and just hold the feeling. You'll be amazed at how good it'll be if you wait. Just watch. That's what you want, isn't it? To watch, and let Meinrad and Finn do the work.'

Jill tried to relax and breathe quietly, but Meinrad and Finn certainly weren't breathing quietly. They weren't being quiet at all. Finn ran a fisted hand up and down the length of Meinrad's expanding erection, and Meinrad cupped his balls and squirmed on the sofa. 'God, I'm full,' Meinrad said with a hard grunt and a thrust upward into Finn's fist. 'I've been hard ever since last night. You owe me, Finn. You owe me big time for not letting me shag Jill after all my efforts.'

'I'm paying you back now, mate,' Finn said, rising to kiss Meinrad's mouth like he'd eat his face off. From where she was Jill could see Finn's white-knuckle grip around the girth of the monster cock, and Jesus, it looked like a missile ready to go off at any minute. A quiver ran through Jill's sex and suddenly she felt as though Eleanor's face was pressed to her pout, close to her arousal, as though she were a lab experiment, and Eleanor the professor in charge. In her mind's eye she could almost picture the demon opening her with feminine fingers, examining her, testing her wetness, tasting her, smelling

123

her. 'Don't come,' Eleanor whispered against the swell of her clit. 'Wait. Hold it. Delight in it.'

The pressure of Jill's thighs against each other made her feel heavier, tighter. She opened her legs for relief and took shallow breaths, struggling to hold back. On the sofa, the two men were now vying for position. Finn had lost his T-shirt and Meinrad was shoving at his jeans. There was the sound of shoes dropping onto the wood floor and another scramble of hard male bodies, cocks and clenching bottoms beautifully displayed against the backdrop of her turquoise sofa. It felt like Eleanor was stretching her now, rubbing and scissoring up inside her, and the feeling would have been painful if she hadn't already been so deliciously open, so incredibly responsive to the sight of Meinrad's enormous erection.

There was another mad shuffle on the sofa. Finn stood briefly and rearranged himself so that he straddled Meinrad with his bottom over the man's face. Then he shifted his hips and manoeuvred until Meinrad was able to take his erection into his mouth. Deep into his mouth. Finn made no tempt to hide the grunt of pleasure, nor did he hold back the curse that slipped between his parted lips as Meinrad reached to caress his balls. The exquisite sound of aroused male flesh made Jill slick and needy, which delighted Eleanor until it felt like she vibrated with excitement just below Jill's skin.

Once Finn had settled into position with his penis deep

in Meinrad's throat, he lowered himself down over the man's belly and wriggled and shifted until he was able to take the jut of Meinrad's erection into *his* mouth, and Jill was stunned at just how much of it he was able to take. She could see the muscles of Meinrad's belly tense and bulge and tense again as Finn slid the O of his open lips down the shaft and back up again, his cheeks pulling tight in his efforts.

Almost without realising it, Jill unbuttoned her blouse and stood with her legs open, slit clenching like it had a mind of its own. She caressed her breasts, shifting from foot to foot, struggling to keep her hands away from her crotch as she watched the fascinating scene unfolding on the sofa.

Once again the two rearranged themselves, and Meinrad bent over the couch with his legs apart, his backside griping and relaxing, gripping and relaxing. With his penis leading the way, Finn moved behind him, kissing and nipping down the big man's spine and onto his butt cheeks, which he kneaded and licked and separated in strong hands. His tongue and lips trailed their way to the deep crevice in between to place a kiss and a stroke upon Meinrad's dark hole before Finn began to press and circle, press and circle with his tongue.

'Fuck,' Meinrad hissed between his teeth, grabbing onto the bounce of his penis with a tight fist as though he were about to downshift.

As Finn replaced his tongue with the probe and scissor of two fingers, Meinrad groaned. 'I want her, Finn. Let me have her.'

'Shut up, Meinrad.' Finn shoved wriggling fingers in hard and then Meinrad grunted and pushed back against him.

'You owe me,' he breathed.

'I don't owe you anything,' Finn said. Then he spat on his hand, lubed his cock with his saliva and thrust it in hard. Meinrad bucked and roared loud enough to rattle the windows.

The violence of the act caught Jill by surprise and she let out a sharp little yelp before she managed to cover her mouth with her hand. But it was too late. There was no taking it back.

Finn's spine stiffened, and Jill could see his buttocks tense from where he stood. Her heart raced at the sight of him buried to the hilt in another man's butt. It was something she'd never seen before, something so raw and sexual that she felt as though her own insides were being abraded in empathy. Finn gave a hard thrust, then cursed. 'Goddamn it, Jill, come here.'

Her heart felt like it was suddenly in free-fall as she stumbled forward into view, waiting for reassurance from Eleanor that didn't come.

'Here.' He motioned her to his side, next to where he stood, deep inside Meinrad. 'Right here.'

126

On unsteady legs she moved to stand by Finn, so close she could hear his breath with each thrust, so close she could smell the scent of his arousal and the way his scent blended with the sharper, more piquant smell of Meinrad's heat.

'I want you to suck Meinrad,' he said.

Meinrad pushed back hard against Finn and dislodged him. 'Bloody hell, Finn, I don't want her to suck me off. I want her to fuck me.'

The little whimper that escaped Jill's throat was involuntary, and she sat down hard on the couch. Both men stood facing each other, completely naked, sweat-sheened chests heaving, cocks raised like swords, breathing like they were already fighting a duel.

'You stupid bastard, you'll hurt her, can't you see that?' The words tumbled out of Finn's mouth and swirled around Jill, making her dizzy. Inside her, she thought she could feel Eleanor positively trembling with anticipation.

'No.' Jill forced the word up her tight throat. 'No, it's all right. I don't mind.' She held Finn's gaze. 'If you don't.'

'But that's the problem, love,' Meinrad breathed. 'Can't you tell? He does mind.'

Finn surprised her by pulling her to her feet into a desperate kiss, pressing himself against the fabric of her flip skirt. Then he held her gaze, his eyes like fire. 'It's not Eleanor, is it? It's not her pushing you to shag Meinrad?'

She shook her head and for some reason, some reason

she couldn't quite figure, she said, 'Finn, I'll do what you want me to. Whatever you ask.' This time Eleanor was positively purring.

'I don't want him to hurt you.'

'Fuck, Finn, I can control myself,' Meinrad said. 'You know I can. I would never hurt her. Not unless she wanted me to.'

'Finn, tell me what to do,' Jill said. Inside, it felt almost like Eleanor was shivering with delight.

Finn pulled her close and held her there against the rise and fall of his chest. 'You can shag Meinrad, Jill, but I want to be in control.' He shot Meinrad a warning glance. 'I want to be in control.'

Meinrad looked from Finn to Jill, then back again, his hand fisted around his straining erection. Then he nodded his consent. 'You're the coven leader.' He reached out his hand to Jill.

In a move not unlike last night, Finn took Jill's hand and offered it to Meinrad.

Still holding her gaze, Meinrad raised her fingers to his lips and kissed them. 'I won't hurt you, Jill. I want to make love to you. I want to make you feel good.' He stepped forward carefully, as though he were afraid he might frighten her, then he engulfed her in an enormous embrace that felt all-encompassing, but somehow neither suffocating nor frightening.

Finn stepped in close behind, so close she could feel

him hard up against her. Then he slipped the shirt off over her shoulders and pulled her back against his chest, opening a space between her and Meinrad, enough space for Meinrad to inspect her breasts, dwarfing them in his large hands, large hands that had bound her with delicate knotwork only the night before.

'Yes,' he sighed, settling a kiss against her sternum. 'Yes.'

She ran her hand over the soft cap of white-blond hair and held him to her. With a palm placed against the curve of her jaw, Finn turned her just enough that his mouth could take hers in a kiss that was slow, leisurely, almost lazy. Than he pulled her back against him and settled them both on the floor, his spine resting against the sofa, hers against him. Meinrad followed them down, caressing her breasts and running a hand over her belly.

As they lay against the couch, the hand on her abdomen continued its migration down over her pubic curls, down to the splay of her, to breach her with thick index and middle fingers.

Finn placed his hands under her bottom and lifted, shoving the skirt out of the way, positioning her so that her bare feet rested on his thighs, effectively thrusting her upward and opened for Meinrad's inspection. And her own seaside scent joined the rising tide of pheromones. Meinrad's groan of approval was warm between her thighs. He fingered his way deeper to stroke and press her G-spot just as Finn pried her open further with the kneadings of his hands on her buttocks. The flood of her arousal soaked Meinrad's fingers.

'Fuck,' he whispered, moving in close enough to lick and nip at the open gape of her around his fingers.

'Fuck,' she repeated, as the first orgasm nearly dislodged her from Finn's firm grip and had Meinrad grabbing for his erection, thumbing the head of it hard.

Finn wriggled from under her and eased her gently back on the floor, while Meinrad kept stroking, and her body kept gripping and convulsing in the aftershocks. Both men sat on their haunches, faces close, to watch the quivering and trembling of her personal landscape, like her own private earthquake, she thought.

'I need to take her, soon,' Meinrad said, his voice gravelly and rough with arousal. 'I've been hard for her since last night.'

'Not yet,' Finn said. 'Another finger. Stretch her a little more.' One of Finn's hands had migrated up to her breasts and was pinching, kneading and tweaking. The other gripped his own erection as though he were afraid it might escape him if he let go. 'Just a little more, Jill. Just a little more,' he said. 'Then I'll let Meinrad put his cock in you.' He leaned forward and kissed her nipples.

It was all she could do to hold still. It was all she could do to keep from bucking off the floor. She thrashed and moaned beneath Meinrad's expert ministerings. 'That's my girl.' The big man's voice was little more than a breathless gasp. 'That's my lovely demon girl, so soft and slick and ready for me. That's my nasty little Jill. Do you have room in your slippery little pussy for me?' He gave his penis a solicitous tug at the same time as he thrust his fingers up into her hard, and she shivered with pleasure.

'Hold her bottom for me, Finn,' Meinrad said. 'I can't wait any longer. I need to be inside her. Now.'

This time, Finn didn't argue. He returned to his former position, pressed between her back and the sofa, and, with his hands cupped under her buttocks, positioned her so that she was presented to Meinrad like a slippery wet gift. 'It's all right,' he whispered against her nape, laving her with kisses. 'Meinrad'll make love to you now, and it may hurt a little when he first pushes into you. But then, Jill, then it'll feel so good. So very good.'

With Finn whispering in her ear and caressing her bottom and Eleanor quivering with excitement that Jill felt through every nerve ending, Meinrad positioned himself. He spat heavily on his hand for extra lubrication. Not that she wasn't ready to accommodate him, but he was big, and until two nights ago the largest object she'd had inside her was a dildo that had been dwarfed by Finn's penis, let alone Meinrad's missile.

The stretching began at her opening and spread up the length of her vagina like a flash fire. All breath left her. Her eyes watered, her buttocks clenched. She wasn't sure it was Eleanor egging her on, or if it was just her need to feel all of Meinrad's penis, but she kept pushing herself onto the length of him, while Finn spoke quietly to her, words that registered only as sound above her straining. Meinrad entered her a centimetre at a time with little undulations of his hips, not enough to be thrusts, but just enough to squeeze into her a little further and a little further and a little further until he was in all the way. For a long moment he held very still. No one in the room was breathing. Jill wasn't sure she could have if she'd wanted to.

And then, he arched up over her body. With a long laving of his tongue up each side of her cheek he licked away the tears that had resulted from the pressure of his mounting. Then he gave the first bruising thrust. Then another. Then another. And somewhere between thrusts her breath returned to her. Finn's words of encouragement made sense again. And she felt Eleanor's excitement flash up her spine. Then, with a growl that didn't sound like it could have come from her throat, she wrapped her legs around Meinrad's waist and thrust up to meet him.

She was concentrating so hard on the burgeoning of another orgasm that she barely noticed Finn wriggle from beneath her until she heard him grunt, and felt Eleanor's delight as he pushed back into Meinrad. The big man sucked a harsh breath in response, but never missed a beat in his hammering of Jill's sex.

The mesmerising rhythm of the three of them thrusting and retreating, thrusting and retreating together, built and expanded until it reached the point of no return and they all tumbled over the edge into orgasm like dominoes, Jill going first, pulling Meinrad along with her just as Finn grunted his release into Meinrad. For the briefest moment, Jill was certain she could feel Eleanor expanding within her to fill every single lust-heated cell of her body and even more beyond. For a second, Jill felt like she could no longer be contained within the walls of her own flat, within the walls of her building, within the expanse of London that was Shoreditch. Just when fear threatened the experience, she found herself back on the floor of her lounge crushed beneath the two men, sweaty and wet and drowsy from seriously hot sex, demon-possessed sex.

But before she could settle into post-coital bliss, Finn broke the spell. 'I need a shower.' He stood quickly, and Jill felt as though something had been ripped from her.

'Shit,' Meinrad said, as they watched him disappear into the bathroom.

'He's jealous,' Eleanor said softly. 'That's all. He's jealous. Don't worry, Jill. He'll get over it.'

'But I thought he wanted me to ... us to, or I never would have,' Jill said out loud.

Meinrad placed a kiss on her cheek, then sat up and

began to dress. 'He doesn't know what the hell he wants since you came into the picture, love. And anyway, I shouldn't have asked. It's just that it's never been like this before. He was never like this with Lisa.'

Inside her, it was as though Eleanor had just convulsed. She felt a tidal wave of emotions that nearly took her breath away. But she spoke over the discomfort. 'Lisa? Did Eleanor possess her?'

Meinrad looked suddenly pale, paler even than he usually was. 'Look, Jill, I have to go. I didn't mean to cause problems. I'm sorry.' As she stood to walk him to the door, he placed a quick kiss on her cheek and hurried to let himself out, leaving her standing in nothing but her mussed skirt in the middle of her lounge. Somewhere in the back of her mind, she heard the shower come on.

'Go back to bed,' Eleanor said softly. 'He'll be all right. You'll see.'

She was too tired to argue with Eleanor, and sleep would be a far better way of coping with the swirl of emotions she felt right now than angsting them out while waiting for Finn to get over it. She suspected that Eleanor might be giving her just a little nudge in the sleep department, but she was OK with that at the moment.

She didn't know how much later it was when Finn slipped into bed next to her and pulled her possessively into a spoon position. Or perhaps she only dreamed it.

# Chapter 12

'I wasn't comfortable with it. I wasn't at all comfortable with it,' Finn was saying.

'It was beautiful. It was exquisite for all of us,' came Eleanor's reply. 'And I've never felt you come so hard.'

There was a long silence, in which Jill realised, once again, that she was dreaming. This time they were in her bedroom. Like before, Eleanor was using her body, lying there on the bed next to Finn. And Jill, well, she was bound, just like she had been in the previous dream. Only this time, Jesus, this time she was bound and suspended above her own bed, like a giant bird, arms tied behind her back, legs bent and open wide. She was just high enough that if either of them reached out to her they would have been able to touch her with their fingertips. But they didn't seem to notice her there at all.

'I think you came so hard because you were

uncomfortable with the situation,' Eleanor said, leaning in and brushing a kiss across his stubbled cheek.

'You can think what you want,' Finn said. 'He could have hurt her.'

'Oh, now you're just being ridiculous. You know that he wouldn't hurt her. Meinrad above all the people in Sole Alliance knows how not to hurt someone if they don't want to be hurt. Though I'm not entirely sure our Jill doesn't like being hurt, at least just a little bit.'

Finn didn't respond this time, and for a second Jill wondered if he'd fallen back asleep. Then Eleanor said. 'It's not that you don't want Meinrad to hurt her, Finn. It's that you don't want anyone else to have her. Why don't you admit it?' She leaned close to his ear and Jill had to strain to hear what was said. 'But you melted when she asked your permission. Don't think I didn't notice that. You want to control her.'

'Damn right, I want to control her. If she asks my permission for everything she does, sexually I mean, then maybe she'll stay safe.'

Jill shivered in her elegantly knotted web, and a picture of another woman suspended flashed like a ruptured after-image through her head. It was already past before she realised this woman had not been tied lovingly by another. This woman had tied the knot herself, a slip-knot around her neck, done in a moment of despair, done before anyone could stop her.

Then Jill's nest of knots gave way beneath her, tumbling her back into her body. She cried out and pushed at the duvet.

It took her a second to reorient herself to the bed she was no longer above, to the arms of Finn now wrapped protectively around her. 'Jill, Jill! Wake up. Are you all right?' In the darkened room she felt his gaze more than saw it, but it felt grounding, a strange word she never would have used before her association with Eleanor and the Sole Alliance. She laid her head against his chest. 'It's all right It was just a dream. I'm fine. I'm OK.'

He pulled her close to him, forcing a little grunt from her with his enthusiasm. 'You scared me,' he said. 'You seemed so distressed.'

'I'm all right,' she replied. But somehow the discomfort of the dream lingered.

Finn was already gone in the morning when she woke up.

* * *

Her arrival at the office on Monday morning was greeted with relief. 'Mrs Kenny wants to see you, in Mr Devlin's office,' the receptionist said, shifting nervously in her seat.

'What's going on?' Jill asked. Mrs Kenny was Devlin's superior, and Jill had only ever met the woman once in the three years she'd been working at *Full On*.

'No idea.' The receptionist avoided her gaze and shifted

137

the few items on her desk as though she were attempting to look busy.

Inside Devlin's office, Jill was instantly aware that something was wrong. The man's personal items were gone and the office was empty.

'Sit down, Jill.' The well-preserved Mrs Kenny wore a mauve power suit that had expensive written all over it, and before Jill had completely settled in the chair the woman began. 'Mr Devlin has left us.'

Jill barely managed to utter a little gasp of surprise before the woman waved her hand as though she were shooing away a mosquito. 'It was sudden. Personal problems of some type, but, for whatever reason, he felt it most urgent that he leave immediately.' Mrs Kenny folded her hands on top of the bare desk and held Jill in a cast-iron stare. 'I'm sorry for the man's problems, Jill, as I'm sure you can imagine, but I still have a business to run, and I'm not blind to the fact that a good deal of what gets done around here is getting done by you.' The woman straightened her jacket and looked down at her watch. 'There should be a meeting of staff to plan this week's eZine this morning, am I right?'

She didn't wait for Jill's reply. 'Certainly I'm not informed enough on events and long-term plans to run that meeting, Jill, but I know you are. And you're probably more qualified than Devlin was to run this eZine. That means you'll have to pick up the slack, straighten up the mess Devlin left and get things back up to speed.'

Jill was about to tell her that she had only come in to talk to HR about her severance, but then it hit her. Devlin hadn't told anyone about her quitting. He'd opted to just leave. Technically she was still employed at *Full On*, and her reason to quit was no longer there.

'The job's yours, Ms Hart.'

That got her attention. And when Jill did nothing more than offer a gasp of surprise, Mrs Kenny raised an eyebrow. 'Well? What are you waiting for? Once the planning meeting's over see HR about your new employment status and have them change the name on the door. I'll have my secretary schedule a lunch for us in two weeks, and we can discuss your vision for *Full On*. I'm excited to see what you can do.'

She stood and offered Jill her hand. 'Good luck, Ms Hart. By the way, I enjoyed your busker story.' Then she turned and left, closing the door to Jill's office behind her, leaving Jill to try and catch up with what had just happened. Meanwhile Eleanor did a fine job of demon smug that made Jill feel, well, not exactly orgasmic, but pretty fucking close.

\* \* \*

Being in charge at *Full On*, as Jill suspected, wasn't an easy task. And it was not made easier by the disarray Devlin had left it in. She had managed a quick text to Vivie and to Finn filling them in on her new employment status. Vivie had answered back almost immediately with excited congratulations. Finn, on the other hand, had not replied.

Fortunately she had been too busy to dwell on the absence of a response from Finn, and by what should have been the end of the day Jill was beginning to realise that it really wasn't going to be the end of the day. Not that she minded. She was up for the challenge. She had fantasised more than once about what she would do if the reins of power ever got wrenched from that wanker Devlin's hands and turned over to her. She just never really believed it would happen. Still, that meant when five o'clock came she was hard at work, and when six rolled around, she was no closer to leaving. Up to her elbows in stuff that should have been done last Friday, she whipped off a quick text to Finn.

*Have to work late. Will be home as soon as I can. J*

It was nearly seven, and she was about to leave when her BlackBerry rang. It was Finn.

'Where the hell are you, Jill? I've been looking all over for you. This is no joke. Who are you with? What the fuck does Eleanor have you doing?'

Her stomach knotted and she felt as though she'd been slapped. 'What do you mean, who am I with? Didn't you get my text? I told you I'm at the office. I had to work late. I've been –'

He cut her off. 'I thought you were quitting. And now all of a sudden you're the boss? What did she do? What did Eleanor do?'

'My boss quit and I took his job, arsehole. I took his job because I'm the person qualified, and I'm the person his boss put in charge. And since when has being civil become such a difficult task?' She disconnected before the situation could escalate. 'Wanker!' She said under her breath as she slammed her laptop shut and shoved everything into her bag. 'What the hell happened to being polite? Is that so difficult to do? Did he bother to text me back and ask me what was up? Did he bother to call me and clear up the misunderstanding, to congratulate me, to even check in on me? No. He just bites my head off.'

'He was worried,' Eleanor said.

Just then her BlackBerry signalled a text. It was from Finn.

*Sending Chelsea to yours to look after you. Don't know what time I'll be in.*

*F*

She fired back.

*I don't need a child-minder. Give Chelsea the night free and fuck off to wherever you want.*

*J*

As she sent it off, she said. 'I don't want to hear it, Eleanor. It's been a long day.'

She got the equivalent of a shrug. Then she added,

'Clearly he's not all that worried about me or he wouldn't be sending someone else. And who knows where the hell he's getting off to?'

'What you need is a drink at Juno,' Eleanor said. 'Maybe a glass of fizz to celebrate your promotion.'

Jill squared her shoulders. 'That's a good idea. That's exactly what I need, to celebrate. Let's go.'

* * *

At the Water Poet, Finn was halfway through his second pint by the time he'd got the whole sordid story off his chest. Meinrad ordered another lime and soda and leaned against the bar. 'That didn't go too well.'

'I don't need a lecture, Meinrad,' Finn said. 'I know that didn't go too well. Is Chelsea on her way?'

'She's not happy about it,' Meinrad said. 'Whatever's going on between the two of you, you and Jill, I mean, if it doesn't have anything to do with Eleanor then it doesn't have anything to do with Sole Alliance. You know that.'

Finn stared down into his pint. 'Yeah, I know, mate, but I've got to have some time to think. I didn't expect this. And last night when you … when you made love to her …' He ran a hand through his hair and blew out a sharp breath. 'I mean it was just sex, wasn't it? And she was all right with it. And it was good for her. I could tell that it was. You made sure that it was.' That she had been fine with fucking another man right there in front of him, even with his permission, still burned like fire in the pit of Finn's stomach. And that he had not been fine with it burned even worse.

Meinrad made no reply.

'Eleanor's right,' Finn said.

'About what?'

'I don't want anyone else touching her. I don't want anyone else touching Jill.'

'Oh, that,' Meinrad replied. 'I think you were the only one who hadn't figured that out, mate.'

'When she told me she was at work, when she told me about the promotion, all I could think about was what Eleanor had done to get her that promotion. I didn't even text her back, I was so angry. I thought ...'

'You thought Eleanor knew who she had to fuck to get the position and made it happen.'

It sounded really stupid when Meinrad said it, but that was pretty much it.

'Jill doesn't really seem the type for that,' Meinrad said. Then he sipped his lime and soda. 'Still, I suppose she might have a go at Chelsea if you leave them alone together and she's angry enough, which she probably is.' He shook his head. 'She has quite a temper. What a revenge fuck that would be. Might stop by myself – if nothing else, just to watch.'

Finn flipped him off.

'You're a fool, Finn. If the woman were interested in anyone else, she wouldn't look like she does every time she sees you.'

'Look like she does?' Finn said. 'Like how?'

Meinrad downed the rest of his drink and stared into his glass. 'Like you're the only person in the room, or at least the only person she can see.'

A bout of raucous singing erupted at the bar and the two scooted a little further away. Finn downed the rest of his pint and realised that Meinrad was giving him the evil eye.

'What?'

'Finn –' Meinrad leaned closer to be heard over the singing '– Jill's not Lisa. She's not anything like Lisa. Surely you can see that? What happened with Lisa won't happen with Jill.'

'We don't know that, do we? We don't know what will happen when Eleanor leaves Jill, or even if Eleanor stays. Maybe what happened with Lisa always happens. Maybe it's the result of being possessed by a several-thousand-year-old lust demon. Maybe ...'

'Maybe lots of things, Finn. But there's no going back now, is there? And you won't let what happened to Lisa happen to Jill, none of us will, now that we know. I promise you.'

Finn wiped his hands on his jeans and pulled a deep breath. 'It's just that Eleanor can be so ...'

'Eleanor's fine, mate. Eleanor's in good hands with Jill.

Jill's not a pushover, and Eleanor's not stupid enough to make the same mistake.'

'Isn't she? She was stupid enough to risk it all again, wasn't she? Stupid enough to throw caution to the wind, even after everything that happened with Lisa.'

'People get impulsive when they're lonely,' Meinrad said.

'Eleanor's not a person, and besides she has us.'

Meinrad raised an eyebrow. 'With that kind of attitude towards her, I'd say it's no wonder she went looking.' Before Finn could respond, Meinrad raised a hand. 'Listen, mate, it's complicated, I know that. We all know that or we wouldn't be fit to do what we do. But as far as I can tell, Eleanor's fine. Jill's fine. Jill's exquisite, in fact. The only one who's not fine is you.'

The two sat listening to the sound of glasses clinking, and the usual Monday-evening pub noises, calmer than weekends, but never truly quiet.

At last Finn spoke. 'You think I should go find her?'

'She just got a big promotion and you were a twat. You figure it out.' Meinrad looked down at his watch. 'I've got a date to tie a woman up, or do you need me to come hold your hand?'

\* \* \*

'You alone?'

Jill was startled to look up into the eyes of Rugby

Man, leaning on the bar beside her. She hadn't noticed him sidling in next to her. She had to catch herself before she said no. She was, after all, never alone any more. 'Yep, alone. You?'

'I came here with some friends,' he said. 'Just for a few laughs, you know?' He nodded to her glass. 'You're drinking fizz. Special occasion?'

'Big promotion,' she said. Inside Eleanor felt way more reticent than she had last time Rugby Bloke was in the picture. But hadn't she said he was OK? And he did seem nice enough. If he wanted to shag her, well, so what? Isn't that really what most people were looking for? And the other night, had it only been such a short time ago? Back then she might have possibly considered it. But now, now when she should have taken a bit of pleasure in the idea of making Finn jealous, in the idea of shagging Rugby Bloke's brains out, she didn't have the heart for it.

He ordered her another fizz without asking, and himself a Stella. She didn't protest. 'Seems strange to be celebrating something like that alone. It was a good promotion, wasn't it?'

She forced a smile. 'A really good one, actually, and totally unexpected.'

He nodded sagely. 'Well, that explains why you're here alone then. It was so unexpected you haven't had the chance to share the good news.'

Inside she felt Eleanor bristle.

'You said he was a nice guy.'

The man offered her a very kissable smile and gave a quick glance around. 'Who's a nice guy?'

Jesus! She hadn't missed the cues on what should be said out loud and what shouldn't since her first day with Eleanor. A sign of her lousy mood, she reckoned. She smiled back at the man and opted for honesty. 'I'm talking to my demon. She said you're a nice guy.'

Eleanor gave her the equivalent of a demon elbow to the ribs and Rugby Guy cocked his head, then chuckled softly. 'Well, I'd say your demon has good taste, but then I might be a bit prejudiced.'

Eleanor was positively glaring at her.

'What do you want me to do?' she asked.

The man looked slightly confused then said, 'Well, I was about to ask you to dance, but then, wait a minute, are you talking to me or to your demon?'

When Eleanor did nothing but glare at her harder, she said. 'Well, actually I was asking my demon, but she's not a lot of help at the moment, though she seems to have done a fine job of fucking up my life recently.' She straightened her jacket and squared her shoulders. 'Look, you seem like a really nice bloke, and I see a half a dozen women with their eyes on you right now. Truth is, I'm not fit company at the moment, and trust me, you don't want to hear it. But if you came here for a few laughs, I'm not the one to have them with.'

He ran a hand along the square line of his jaw and studied her. 'I might be able to cheer you up.'

'Possibly, but I'm not sure I want to be cheered up at the moment.'

He surprised her by leaning in and kissing her. It wasn't a heavy kiss. It was just a brush across her lips. 'I can be miserable with you if you'd like that better.'

'I wouldn't wish that on anyone,' she said. 'And while I appreciate the offer, I still have to decline. And I really do appreciate the offer. It's just, well, the timing's wrong.'

\* \* \*

Finn didn't hear any of Jill's conversation. All Finn saw through the crowd was Jill in a lip lock with the bloke she'd been dancing with the first time he'd pulled her out of Juno. And he saw red.

He pushed his way through the milling crowd to where the two stood at the bar, and he didn't waste time on preliminaries. 'Goddamn it, Eleanor, what are you doing, just trying to get her hurt?'

Rugby Bloke straightened and squared his shoulders, half moving in front of Jill protectively. 'You're Eleanor?' he spoke over his shoulder, keeping a wary eye on Finn.

'Eleanor's my demon,' she said. 'I'm Jill.' Then she shouldered her bag, pushed past the man and stood nose to nose with Finn. 'Fuck you, Finn, and fuck you, Eleanor.

I've had about enough of people and demons controlling my life, so fuck you both. I'm going to do what I want, and it's none of your damn business.'

As an afterthought, she turned and addressed Rugby Bloke. 'Thanks again for the drink. And in future I highly recommend a woman who's not possessed.' Then she elbowed past Finn toward the door.

# Chapter 13

She shoved her way into the street with Finn right behind her, and Eleanor keeping her mouth shut.

'What were you doing with him?' Finn asked.

She turned to face him, bumping into a couple of smokers milling around out front. 'Not that it's any of your goddamn business what I was doing with him, but he bought me a drink and asked me to dance. Now leave me alone.' She pushed past him. This time he grabbed her by the elbow and swung her around to face him.

'That's all?'

'Fuck you!' She jerked away and headed down the street at breakneck pace towards the bus stop, the path in front of her blurring in a mist of tears.

'Jill! Jill, wait.' He caught up to her, nearly ploughing over a couple snogging on a street corner. 'Jill, I'm trying to apologise.'

This time he grabbed her around the waist and practically hauled her off her feet into a quiet alleyway. 'I was

150

looking for you to apologise and I saw you with him, and I lost it, OK, I just lost it. I thought that Eleanor, that you ... that the two of you ...' His voice drifted off, his chest heaved as though it would explode, and she couldn't help herself. She grabbed him by the hair and pulled him to her in a kiss that was more of a head bashing. Her tongue waged battle with his, her teeth raked and nipped at his responsive lips.

'If you're sorry, prove it,' she said when she came up for air, then she guided his hand up under her skirt, slipping aside the crotch of her panties and fumbling until his fingers were where she needed them.

'Jesus!' he whispered, moving closer, his fingers taking over in their manoeuvring toward the warm wet of her.

She grabbed his face and kissed him again, finding her rhythm against his fingers. Then she pulled back enough to speak. 'Eleanor has nothing to do with what I want, Finn Masters. *I* have to do with what I want. I make the choices, goddamn it. I'm not so feeble-brained that I don't know my own mind.'

She heard his fly open and felt the smooth hot skin of his erection against the inside of her thigh. She felt the brick at her back abrade her elbows as he lifted her onto him, pushing into her hard and rough and angry. And she took him that way. Her insides, still tender from Meinrad's attention the night before, gripped and bit at him as though she would never let him go. Her booted feet dug into his kidneys, her nails clawed at his back through his shirt.

It was over almost before it began. She flooded him and he returned the favour, grunting and straining as though each thrust wounded him, as though each breath he drew was agony, agony that she let bloom inside her until she gave it back to him transformed and they both came like the world would end.

He didn't settle her back on her feet when they'd finished. He held her there between himself and the wall, whispering her name against the nape of her neck between hot wet kisses. And Eleanor, well, Eleanor seemed somewhere in between. She was not really lodged at Jill's centre where Jill had grown used to her being, but she hadn't completely migrated to Finn's either. She was like ribbon, similar to those in Jill's boots, somehow holding the two of them together and tying strange, demon-shaped knots not unlike Meinrad's handiwork.

When Finn put Jill back on her feet, she found tissues in her bag and they both did their best to clean themselves. He held her possessively on the short bus ride to her house, and she held him back. Neither of them spoke. Eleanor still hadn't moved from her position somewhere in between. Jill would ask Finn about that when she felt like talking again. At the moment, she just felt like being held.

When they finally arrived at her flat, she opened the

door to find a dozen red roses on the coffee table, beside a bottle of champagne resting in a bucket of melting ice. Next to that there was a board with cheese and biscuits and ripe fruit. And her eyes misted. 'You did this?'

He nodded. 'Congratulations on your promotion, Jill. And I'm sorry I was such an arsehole.' Then his ocean-deep eyes were suddenly dark and steamy. 'I hope you'll let me make that up to you.' He raked her with a gaze that she could swear she felt against the tips of her nipples, as though he had sought them out with his lips and tongue. 'I can be very good at apologising properly when given a chance.'

He led her into her room and undressed her slowly, lingering to caress her breasts and her buttocks and stroke the tight nest of curls between her thighs. He took his time to kiss the instep and heel of each foot as he removed her lovely boots. Then he wrapped round her the red silk robe that had been lying across the foot of her bed and led her back into the lounge.

She fed him fat juicy grapes from between the heavy folds of her, which he drizzled with champagne. He tongued and nipped at the fruit bathed in effervescent bubbles, and when he'd extricated each grape he slid up her body and shared it with her, fragrant and juicy with the taste of both of them. When they'd eaten and drunk their fill, they lay spread out naked on the floor. His head rested against her belly, his fingers lazily stroked her pout. 'Why does Eleanor feel like she's halfway between us, not really in either of us?' Jill asked.

'I don't know,' he said, planting a kiss on her navel and sliding up next to her, his fingers still working between her legs. 'Eleanor and I have always been close. She speaks to me, she listens to me, she makes love to me in a way she never really has with Meinrad or Chelsea, though she seems to like them well enough. But I've never shared her with anyone.' He forced an embarrassed chuckle. 'Most of the time I'm too busy just trying to keep her under control.'

'Why?'

He rose on his elbow and looked down into her eyes. 'So she won't hurt anyone, that's why, so she won't … I don't know. So she won't …'

'So she won't leave you?'

Finn didn't respond. But it didn't matter. Suddenly the world was clear in a way it seldom was. Suddenly the mysterious Eleanor was not quite so complicated, and the knowing, the seeing, the understanding sent warm shivers down Jill's spine to pulsate against her clit.

'Finn –' She rose up on her haunches, then knelt next to him. 'What if you didn't control her? What if just for tonight, just now while she has what she wants, you and me together, we let *her* have control. We let her do what she wants with us, what she needs.'

'Jill, I don't think that's a–'

'Sh!' She placed two fingers against his lips and then kissed him. 'It is a good idea. It's the best idea ever.' Even as she said it, in her mind's eye, she could see her self-control binding her as clearly as Meinrad's knots had bound her: right over left and under and through, left over right and under and through. All she needed to do was untie those knots. And for the first time she could see just how to do that. She undid them one at a time, right over left and under and through, feeling the expansion of herself with each loosening, left over right and under and through, until at last she stood, unbound, in bright sunlight, face to face with Eleanor. From somewhere a long way off, she heard Finn moan.

'You love him.' It wasn't a question. Jill knew, just as she knew that for every knot she had untied new ones were already being set in place, and the depth of her binding was beyond anything of which Meinrad was capable.

'You trust me to do this, to love with both of you?' Eleanor said.

'You love him,' Jill repeated. 'You'd never hurt him. Give him this gift.'

From far away, someone touched her arm, and she was back with Finn, and only a second had passed.

'Are you sure?' he asked again.

'Very sure.' The words were barely past her lips before the demon expanded inside her and beyond, taking her

155

breath away, taking Finn's breath away. Her heart pounded in her chest, and the world was suddenly wild and bright and tilting madly at strange new angles, as she straddled Finn, thrusting her hips forward until he could see the whole of her, still heavy from their lovemaking and now glistening with excitement that Eleanor made her feel in every single nerve ending of her body. Then she slid back, raking her open cleft down the length of him until she reached his erection. But then she lifted her bottom and slid still lower until she could take him into her mouth, deep into her throat, pulling, tugging, suckling, running her tongue over the sensitive underside. And it was also Eleanor's tongue, infused with Eleanor's power to heighten sensation. Finn arched his back as though it would break, sucking oxygen into empty lungs, crying out with some wild mix of pain and pleasure a hair's-breadth away from being too much to bear. But he bore it, revelled in it, writhed in it, fingers curled tightly in Jill's hair, muscles tense, joints stiff.

'Finn, my Finn, my beautiful Finn –' Surely it was Eleanor who spoke, and yet it felt like it came from a place in Jill's heart she'd never dared look into before. 'Finn, my Finn.' But there had been no words, no real words. How could there be words when Finn's penis was deep in her throat?

Sliding her mouth up the length of him, she pulled away, then rose on her knees and mounted him. He placed his hands on her hips and guided her deeper and deeper until all of him was sheathed inside her. Every inch of him was alive with Eleanor just beneath his skin, just beneath both their skins, drawing them together, drawing them deeper into each other, tightening their bonds like so many unseen knots.

When he began to thrust, it was as though she rode him from a high place, far away and yet at the same time nearer than the beating of his heart. And Eleanor was there all around them, everywhere. 'I want to stay inside you for ever.' The words were Finn's, but the sentiment could have been anyone's as they rolled and tumbled on the hardwood floor, slick with sweat, tight with passion. When they came, the explosion of lust blew the world apart and then collapsed back in on itself into gasping, writhing, trembling, weak, vulnerable flesh.

* * *

At some point they ate again then stumbled to the bed. Jill couldn't remember how many times she had come, and through it all she felt Eleanor and Finn as though they were one, as though all three of them were one.

Resting her head against the strong steady beat of Finn's heart, Jill tried to take in the events of the past few hours. Unable to, she placed a kiss on the rise and fall of his sternum and said, 'She loves you, you know. Eleanor does.'

She felt him nod. 'I know,' he said. Then he lifted her chin so she could see his eyes shining dark in the waning moonlight filtering through her window. 'That's why she took you. For me.'

Before she could respond to his words with anything more than the skittering of her insides, he kissed her very softly. 'Now go to sleep, Jill. We both have to work tomorrow, and we've got lots of time to talk about our little ménage.'

# Chapter 14

'We've never done anything like that. You and I,' Finn said.

'I've always wanted us to. It was always my plan.' Eleanor replied.

Jill was dreaming again, but this time she wasn't tied up. This time she stood quietly at the side of her bed looking down at the couple. Eleanor rested her head on Finn's chest, absently stroking a nipple that stood erect against the mound of his pectoral muscle 'I was crushed when things went so badly with Lisa. Surely you know that.' She rose to meet his gaze. 'But it's different with Jill. She's so comfortable. She feels so right. Even you think so, I can sense it every time you touch her.'

Though Jill knew what she looked down on from the hazy place of dreams wasn't real, Eleanor's statement made her chest feel tight, as though some unpleasant thing had worked its way into her lungs and was squeezing them.

159

Finn pulled Eleanor closer to him, into such a tight embrace that Eleanor emitted a little gasp. 'I've never felt anything like what the three of us share,' he said. 'But I'm afraid, Eleanor. I'm so afraid. You could have experienced her through me. You could have left her as she was. I mean, the attraction was there between us before you possessed her, and every time I'm with her I want her more. I don't understand why you risked it.'

'I would have thought that would be obvious, my darling.' Eleanor traced a finger down along Finn's sternum, trailing a ticklish path down beneath the duvet to where his cock rested against his thigh. 'I don't want to experience the world through your body, Finn. I want to experience what it feels like to love your body, the way you like your body to be loved, the way I never can when I'm inside you. You've never been without flesh. You don't understand how it is to feel things you can't express, to watch the world around you and not be able to interact with it unless you ... unless you take up residence in someone who has what you don't, in someone who has flesh and bone and breath.' She slid her hand under his penis and rested it gently against his balls.

He pulled her hand away and brought it to his lips. 'Dear Goddess, Eleanor, I know I don't understand. I can't possibly, but you have to understand what you've done to Jill, what will happen to her when you leave.'

'But we don't know that, Finn. We don't know that.

I'm convinced she'll be just fine. In fact I'm convinced that she ...'

He shook her gently. 'That she what?'

'That she won't want me to leave.'

Jesus! Jill had never thought about asking Eleanor to stay on as a permanent resident, and yet at the moment she couldn't imagine life without her.

'That's one helluva gamble to take after what happened to Lisa,' Finn said.

'What? What happened to Lisa, and what gamble are we taking?' Perhaps she was talking in her sleep. Perhaps she was speaking in the dream, but suddenly she was falling back into her body, and she woke in Finn's arms. 'I want to know. Tell me about Lisa. Tell me about the gamble.'

The startled look on Finn's face was mirrored in the equally startled feel of Eleanor inside her. 'You heard us?' Finn said. His voice sounded breathy, a bit unsteady.

'Of course I heard you. I heard every word.'

'But it was a dream, Eleanor said.'

'Bullshit. It wasn't a dream. You two were talking while I slept, and it's been going on ever since you possessed me, Eleanor.' Jill didn't know how, but she knew. She knew with a gut certainty that Finn and Eleanor's little chats after they thought she was sleeping were exactly that, a chance for them to talk without her hearing.

She thrust her way out from under the duvet and

161

threw on the robe that she had tossed on the floor only a few hours ago. 'Tell me what the hell is going on.' She paced at the side of the bed. 'Who's Lisa? Did she really hang herself? And what's this gamble that I'm suddenly at risk in? And don't lie to me,' she said, 'because I'll know.' She didn't know if she'd know or not, but it felt like she would.

Finn sat up in the bed and settled the duvet over his lap. He worried his bottom lip with his teeth, then he spoke. 'Lisa was the last woman Eleanor possessed.'

'Was?' Jill said, perching on the bed across from him. 'Then she is dead.'

'Yes.' The word was barely more than a whisper, and she didn't miss the rise and fall of his throat as he swallowed, as though even that simple word was painful.

'Hanged herself?'

He nodded.

'Why?'

Finn reached for her hand but she pulled it away.

'Eleanor didn't stay with Lisa as long as she had intended. She thought, Sole Alliance, we all thought that it was too dangerous. We thought that Eleanor facilitated her ... unstable behaviour, so we thought Eleanor should leave before Lisa did something to hurt herself or someone else. We couldn't contain her behaviour within Sole Alliance, and Eleanor ...'

'I thought I should give her free rein, and, in truth, I

delighted in all the things she did, all the dangerous things we did together.' It was almost as though Eleanor moved closer to Jill, trying to make sure Jill understood. 'There were orgies, drugs, sex with strangers, dangerous strangers. Nothing was too extreme for Lisa with me in residence, and it wasn't just sex, it was anything, anything risky, anything dangerous, and I felt it all, all the excitement, all the fear, all the debauchery, things I'd never been allowed to feel under the control of Sole Alliance. You need to understand I've been under the control of Sole Alliance for a very long time. Finn and his gang are just the latest incarnation. And Finn, well, Finn has been much kinder to me. But that didn't make me any better behaved.'

'So you were exorcised from Lisa?' Jill asked, not allowing herself to be pulled into the demon's remorse, which felt way too much like her own.

'There was no need to. I came out willingly. There was a death. She was doing rope play with one of her lovers. She wasn't nearly as skilled at it as Meinrad is.'

'Jesus,' Jill whispered, suddenly feeling cold, as though she would never be warm again.

'After that, I left her. I thought, we all thought, she'd calm down after I left. We never imagined that ...'

'That she'd kill herself.'

Finn nodded.

'I've never possessed anyone I intended to leave willingly. That only happened under the control of Sole

Alliance, and before Lisa, well, before Lisa my last possession was nearly a hundred years ago.'

'Did she die? The person before Lisa?' Jill was trembling, but she pushed Finn away again when he reached for her. 'Well, did she?'

She felt Eleanor's slight nod of confirmation as though the earth had shaken beneath her. She swayed on the bed, then grabbed onto the night stand at her side to steady herself, to keep the world in focus, to keep herself grounded. For an eternal moment, her world consisted of breathing in and breathing out. Right over left and under and through. Left over right and under and through. And when she was at last able to speak again, she felt calm growing at her centre, and it came from a place where Eleanor was not. 'Then when you leave me, I'll die.'

'We don't know that,' both Finn and Eleanor said at the same time.

'We don't know that at all,' Eleanor said. 'You're different. You're not like the others. You're certainly not like Lisa.'

When she was sure her legs would support her, she cinched a knot in the sash of her robe, then stood and turned to face Finn. In her mind's eye, she was also facing Eleanor. 'If you left Lisa at will, then I'm assuming the whole ritual, all of that stuff in Finn's basement, was as much of a lie as everything else, and that you can leave me whenever you like. Is that true?'

"Jill, you have to understand the risks. What we were doing that night in the basement could have –'

'Is that true?' she cut him off.

Once again both Finn and Eleanor nodded confirmation. Then Finn spoke. 'But that might have been the problem with Lisa. Maybe if we'd waited. Maybe –'

'Eleanor, I want you out. Now.'

She heard the startled silence inside her head.

Finn practically catapulted out of the bed, came to her side and took her arm. 'Jill, please. We can work this out. Give us a chance.'

She jerked away. 'I said I want her out now. I've got a hard day ahead of me, a hard week. If I die, I want to do it on my terms, not because you two toyed with my life like it was a fucking pair of shoes at your damned store to be filled by the right-sized foot. Now! And I mean it!'

There was a crackle that felt like an electrical current being discharged up her spine. For a second her head felt like it had swollen, like it would explode with all that it contained. Then Finn took her into his arms and kissed her, and she felt his body tense and the sensation, the power, the force that was Eleanor moved back into his body.

Then she was only conscious of pushing him away, stepping back towards the door, feeling as though there were nothing left inside her but a hollow space. 'I'm going to take a shower,' she said. 'I expect you two to be gone by the time I get out, or I'll call the police.' She turned and walked, on surprisingly steady legs, out of the bedroom. Once she was safe in the rising steam of the shower, she wept.

# *Chapter 15*

Vivie nearly beat the door down before Jill could open it. She scooped her in a desperate bear hug. 'Thank God you're all right!' And then she was blubbering on Jill's shoulder.

Before Jill could say anything Vivie spoke, still holding her tight. 'I know,' she said between sobs. 'I know everything. I know about Eleanor; I know about Sole Alliance. Finn told me.'

Jill supposed she should have been furious that Finn had brought Vivie into this mess, but instead she found herself moved, holding her friend to her as though her life depended on it. Vivie's sobs invited her own, which she had managed to stave off through the workday by burying herself in the mountains of unfinished business Devlin had left. There was no need for that now, and the tears came.

After a while they settled on the sofa with a bottle of chardonnay, and Vivie continued. 'You have to take her back, Jill. You have to take Eleanor back. You have to, because you're my best friend and I couldn't stand it if something happened to you. I just couldn't.'

'I made it through the day without dying,' Jill said, 'and I don't have any plans to kill myself.' She chafed her arms with her hands, feeling cold and empty. 'Though I do have an urge to curl up in bed and cry for a few months.'

'Finn's desolate,' Vivie said. 'And so is Eleanor, I'm told.'

'Glad to know I'm in good company.' Jill downed her glass of wine and was about to refill before she remembered that, without Eleanor, she was no longer immune to the effects of alcohol, and she had to work tomorrow. She'd need her wits about her, and work was sanity at the moment. She didn't want to be hungover.

Vivie grabbed her hand and squeezed it till it hurt. 'Bloody hell, Jilly, it's not worth losing your life over, is it? Finn said you and Eleanor got on well. He said you were good together.' She held her gaze. 'He said the three of you were good together. Jilly, the man loves you, can't you see that?'

'How do I know it's really me he loves, Vivie?' Jill pulled her hands away and blew her nose on a mangled tissue. 'I mean, what part do I really play in our little ménage? I'm just the blank slate Eleanor can make over into her own image, into Finn's dream lover.' She wiped fiercely at her eyes. 'If it's just the demon enhancements that make me super-Jill, sexier, smarter, prettier, more fashion-conscious, then it's not really me anyway, is it? It's someone else he loves.'

Vivie shook her head, and the lovely lines of her jaw stiffened as though she were biting something hard. 'You can't really be that stupid, Jilly. Finn wanted you before Eleanor ever took up housekeeping. He told me so. Did it ever occur to you that Eleanor has nothing without flesh? Did it ever occur to you that maybe in you she has everything she wanted, everything she ever dreamed of? You're smart, you're beautiful, you're tender-hearted, you're passionate. Hell, if I could trade places with anyone in the world, it would be you, Jill. Are you the only one who can't see? Are you really the only one who doesn't know how amazing you are?'

She didn't feel amazing. She felt anything but. Not that it mattered. She couldn't see that she had any choice under the circumstances. Jill squared her shoulders and ignored the tears. She figured she'd best get used to them. 'Whether I live or die doesn't matter so much, Vivie, if it's not me. Things were amazing with Eleanor, and I miss her, and I miss Finn. But I have to know. I have to be certain that I'm still Jill Hart, and that it's me, really me that they want.'

*Three Months Later*

'Fizz and not tequila shots. I'll take that as a good sign.' The voice made Jill's insides somersault, and the fact that she somehow knew that Finn Masters wasn't alone, that Eleanor was in residence, made the feeling all the more intense.

'I'm celebrating. *Full On* is one of the most frequently visited eZines in the UK. The list just came out.'

'I know,' he said. 'I've been following it. Its success is mostly due to you, from what I understand. Congratulations.'

He sat down on the stool next to her and ordered a pint. For a second they sat in silence watching the Friday-evening crowd swell the ranks at the Water Poet, almost before their eyes. 'Is Meinrad minding the shop tonight?' she asked, hoping that light and airy conversation would disguise the nerves that bubbled to the surface with Finn and Eleanor so close to her after all these weeks, after all of the agony of trying to get used to being without them.

'Chelsea,' he said. 'Meinrad's off tying up a woman over in Camden Town.'

'And you? You and Eleanor?'

When the bartender brought Finn's pint, he also brought Jill another glass of fizz, and Finn offered her a warm smile. 'We came to help you celebrate. Vivie told us.'

Jill still couldn't imagine how Finn had convinced her friend that none of them were insane. She wasn't sure she could have pulled it off. Ultimately she had been glad to have a friend whose shoulder she could cry on, and she cried on Vivie's shoulder a lot in those early days, a friend who understood exactly the circumstances of her anguish. She reckoned that Vivie was Finn and Eleanor and Sole Alliance's way of having an insider, one whom Jill wouldn't chase away, one who could make sure Jill didn't try to hang herself or jump into the Thames with a breeze-block tied around her neck.

In addition to Vivie's eagle eye, Jill knew that Sole Alliance were keeping watch over her. She never actually saw them, except for the occasional glimpse of someone tall and big as a mountain disappearing around a corner, or a wild mass of dreadlocks that vanished in a crowded Shoreditch street before she got a good look. But what was most reassuring, as well as disconcerting, was the smell. Occasionally, always when she least expected it, always when she most needed it, the scent of Finn that she knew so well would fill the air, so powerfully and so close to her that she expected to turn and find him standing there. He never was. Some sort of Sole Alliance magic, or maybe some demon voodoo that Eleanor conjured up.

She wanted to be angry about the close watch she was sure they kept on her. She wanted to call it stalking. She wanted someone of flesh and blood that she could tell to fuck off. But there was no one, and in truth she found it comforting to think they were keeping an eye on her. She found in it some wild sense of hope that she couldn't fully allow herself and yet couldn't fully deny herself either. And anyway, it could have just as easily been her imagination.

She returned her attention to the sea-water eyes of Finn Masters looking down at her and, with a sudden tightening of her throat, she realised just how much she'd missed them. She smiled up at him. 'Have you come to celebrate me still being alive?'

The smile slipped from his face, but he held her gaze and gave her a slow nod of confirmation. 'Something like that, I suppose.'

She lifted the new champagne flute in a toast. 'I celebrate that every day, Finn. Cheers.' They both drank.

For a long moment they sat next to each other in silence, but it was strangely comfortable silence considering all that had passed between them.

'How's Eleanor?' Jill finally asked, when she'd got the courage.

'I'm fine, Jill.' Hearing Eleanor's voice from Finn's lips was a little disconcerting, but it was Eleanor nonetheless. She knew it was. 'I miss you.'

Jill blinked hard, and the room seemed suddenly misty. 'I miss you too.' The words weren't as strong as she'd intended. They wavered at the back of her throat before they found their way out.

In an act that could have been either brave or stupid, Finn reached out and laid his hand over hers. 'I miss you too, Jill.' His fingers tightened. 'Every second of every day, I miss you.'

Jill bit her lip and swallowed back more emotion than she was ready to give up just yet. But almost as though they had a mind of their own, her fingers curled around his. 'I had to know,' she said. 'I had to know that I could survive without her, that my life didn't depend on her. Or you.'

'I know that.' Finn said. 'I understand that. I always understood that.' He squeezed her fingers until she feared he'd break them, and yet she held on. 'But letting you go, giving you the space you needed, was the hardest thing I've ever done. The hardest thing either of us has ever done.'

She nodded, afraid to speak, not wanting to blubber in such a public place.

Before she could respond, he continued. 'You have to know that giving you space didn't mean I was letting you go, not really letting you go. It never meant that. I have every intention of elbowing my way back into your life. I've just been waiting for the right moment.'

Her insides leapt at his words, almost as though Eleanor were there inside her again, excited, happy, anticipating. She gave a little laugh. 'Now that you know I'm not going to die.'

He took both of her hands and pulled her off the stool to her feet. 'I would have never let you die, Jill.

Surely you know that.' Before she could reply he kissed her. It was quick and awkward and yet she felt Eleanor's excitement mixed with her own, mixed with the dance of nervous hope they all three felt just below the surface in the space that wasn't exactly flesh, the space that was just the right size for a demon.

When he pulled away, she looked down at the mauve boots she wore almost every day. 'I still haven't paid for these, you know.'

He followed her gaze. 'The accumulation of interest alone is staggering.' The corner of his mouth twitched with a repressed smile.

'I always try to pay my debts,' she said.

'It's a big one, and long overdue.' This time he pulled her to stand between his legs where even in the fading light she could see he was hard. They weren't alone in the kiss he pulled her into. It was long and lingering and Eleanor was once again installed comfortably in the space between, the space that still joined them, still felt like it could be filled by no one else but them.

He pulled away breathless. 'Let's get out of here. I want to be alone with you.' He held her gaze. 'Just the three of us.'

This time they made the walk back to Kinky Boots with no groping. This time they walked hand in hand in a space that was filled with tightly controlled anticipation. Jill felt Eleanor's presence as surely as if she once again resided in that mysterious place at her centre, and yet she felt her equally wrapped around Finn, more closely than his own skin.

Once they were inside his flat, inside his room, he unzipped her dress. It was slate blue with mauve pinstripes, sleek and sexy, fitted to the curves of her, curves he ran his hands down over before grabbing the hem of the dress and tugging it off over her uplifted arms.

He caught his breath at the sight of her, silver-grey suspenders grasping the tops of sheer stockings, a bra of matching lace barely covering the jut of her anxious nipples. 'It wasn't you,' she said to Eleanor. 'It wasn't you making me anything I wasn't already. It was just you giving me the courage to trust myself.'

'It's taken you long enough to figure that out,' Finn said. She could tell Eleanor echoed his sentiments. 'All you had to do was ask us. We would have told you.'

When Finn reached to undo her bra, she stopped his hands. 'Tie me up,' she whispered. She brushed a kiss across his stubbled jaw and guided his hands to her breasts. 'I want you to tie me up.'

He led her to the bed, eyes locked on hers as though he were waiting for her to change her mind. When she didn't, he laid her down on the mattress and straddled her so that, where she rested her head on the pillows, the bulge inside his jeans was tantalisingly close to her hungry mouth. With a move that was nothing less than sleight-of-hand, he unhooked her bra and slid it away, dropping a warm kiss on each nipple as he did so. That done, he raised a finger to his lips silencing her. 'Don't speak,' he said. 'Just feel. Just let it happen.' Then he rose once again above her, crossed her hands at the wrist, bound them with her bra and secured them to the brass headboard as high as her arms would stretch.

When he was certain the knot was secure, he lingered to kiss her, and she swallowed his breath, wild, excited, chaotic breath that tasted of him, tasted of lust, tasted of Eleanor. When he pulled away, he rose, still strad-dling her, unbuttoned his shirt and slid it off, revealing the naked rise and fall of his chest, the hard plane of his belly sloping to his navel and to the low ride of his jeans; revealing the long solid muscles of his biceps, the blue-green pathways of the veins running along his forearms beneath smooth skin. And she wanted him like she'd never wanted anything.

Holding her gaze, he lowered a kiss onto her navel. Then he made quick work of her knickers, shimmying them down over her bottom and off, leaving her sex bare and begging, peeking from beneath the lace of the suspenders. As she shifted to get his hand closer to where she needed it, he placed a flat palm against her pubic bone and pressed her back onto the mattress, pausing for a single torturous rake of his thumb against her swelling clit. And she whimpered. But he gave her a warning glance and a finger raised to his lips.

Once she had calmed, once she lay still again, he released a stocking from its suspender and rolled it down over her thigh, down over her calf, down over her ankle, kissing and nibbling as he went. Only the fact that her hands were tied and that he secured the leg he wasn't undressing between his own legs kept her from writhing and squirming with the delight of it, with the nasty pleasure of knowing that each time he bent to kiss her leg, he could easily glance up to admire the view between her legs, slick with the want of him.

Once the stocking was removed, he tied her ankle securely to the brass of the footboard. Then he repeated the act, securing her other leg so that she was splayed open as wide as the footboard would allow.

She was certain he had stretched her out so that she couldn't move, and yet, when he slid out of his jeans and returned to the bed, his erection leading the way, she could see that he had given her just enough moving space for what he had in mind. Then, with one last sleight-of-hand, he removed the suspenders and dropped them to the side of the bed.

She braced herself for his mounting, but instead, he knelt between her legs, one hand resting on his penis, the other moving over her body, caressing her belly, her breasts, the ticklish undersides of her arms. Then he wriggled two fingers up between her the swell of her, into the slick slip and slide of her tight sex, and she gripped them hungrily. His eyelids fluttered at the feel of her, and his breath caught.

'You're bound to me, Jill, bound to Eleanor and me, and I want it that way. I've wanted it that way from the beginning.' He gave a little push with his fingers and she whimpered and jerked involuntarily against her bonds.

Then he leaned low between her legs, holding her open with two fingers, and kissed her opening, mouth wide. His tongue probed and sank deep, his bottom teeth raked as though he would swallow her whole, until his mouth converged and contracted with a tight hard nip and suckle around the erection of her clit. And she convulsed and writhed against his face, grinding her bottom into the mattress, then shifting upwards to get closer.

Breathing like a windstorm, he rose, his face glistening from her, and pushed and manoeuvred until his penis was up tight against her. Then, catching his breath, he spoke. 'You should know that I'm as bound to you as you are to me, that there's no part of me, no part of us, that isn't yours to control, and it's been that way from the beginning.' Then he thrust in hard, and the cry from her throat was raw and desperate and needy in her frustrated efforts to get closer to him.

'Hold still,' he gasped. 'This is mine to give. All mine this time.'

His control was torturous as he pushed all the way in,

then pulled all the way back out, leaving her raw and empty, then pushed all the way back in again.

'Shall I unbind you?' His voice was tight, controlled.

She shook her head wildly. 'No. Don't ever unbind me, Finn. Ever.'

She was sure his eyes were misted with emotion as he took her mouth in a kiss that tasted of her. 'Then we'll come together,' he said. 'All bound together, like we were meant to be.'

She nodded and whimpered, and thrashed against him.

He rose on his knees, cupped her bottom and manoeuvred until he was deep in her pussy, and when he could go no deeper he thrust. He thrust relentlessly. She took him into herself, gripping and grasping and growling, and Eleanor was there in that place in between. She could almost see the knots being tied, she could almost feel the bonding. Right over left and under and through. Left over right and under and through.

They were both too far gone to do anything but hold tight and thrust. His erection seemed to have drilled a hole to her very centre, and she felt as though she could take him into her, take him whole, body and soul. And as they roared their way into orgasm, Eleanor wrapped herself around them, and they all rode the wave of pleasure together.

\* \* \*

Later, when they were lying in each other's arms and Eleanor was curled around both of them, filling all the space in between, Jill asked: 'Eleanor, can she come back to me?'

Finn pulled her still closer and kissed the top of her head. 'If you want her to. But only if you want.'

'I do,' she whispered. 'She belongs in me. It won't be right otherwise. She belongs in me so we can both love you, together.' She blushed as she said it, and yet it felt right.

Finn's response was a bone-crushing bear hug that made her yelp and laugh. 'I can think of nothing I'd rather be than loved by both of you,' he said. And Eleanor's delight shimmered and danced in little ripples around them.

'Will we have to do a ritual?'

'Just the ritual we did the first time, the one in Kinky Boots.' He pulled her on top of him and settled her onto his penis, already hard again. 'All we have to do is lust wildly after each other, and act accordingly.' He was already moving and shifting beneath her, and she was gripping and grinding.

'I think I can manage that,' she said, already anticipating the orgasm that was never far away when she was with Finn and Eleanor.

And that was all it took, just a little lust, a little bumping and grinding, and Eleanor was in. In like Finn.